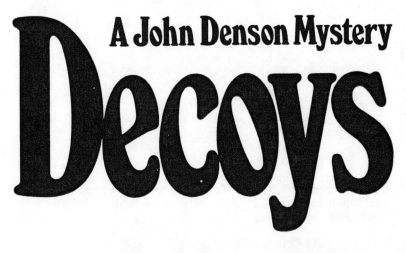

A John Denson Mystery
Decoys

By Richard Hoyt

M. Evans and Company, Inc. New York

Library of Congress Cataloging in Publication Data
Hoyt, Richard, 1941-
  Decoys.
  I. Title.
PZ4.H8685De [PS3558.0975] 813'.54 80-17248
ISBN 0-87131-330-8

M. Evans and Company, Inc.
216 East 49 Street
New York, New York 10017

Design by Diane Gedymin

Manufactured in the United States of America

9 8 7 6 5 4 3 2 1

For Reuel Denney

If you must play, decide upon three things at the start: the rules of the game, the stakes, and the quitting time.

Chinese proverb

One

I DID IT BECAUSE of Sam Spade. I felt part of a tradition of romantic, freelance wise guys. I thought there was no damned woman detective alive who could outsmart John Denson when the old clichéd push came to shove. I'm the first guy at the bar to mouth off about how women are capable of becoming astronauts, brain surgeons, Supreme Court justices, or whatever the hell they want. But dammit, this was different. This was my turf! I knew my stuff.

Understand—I'm not a betting man. I've never played the ponies, slot machines, roulette, craps, poker, or blackjack. I've been to the dogs a couple of times. A big deal for me is to buy a two-dollar show ticket on the track favorite and come away with thirty cents profit, not enough to buy a draught beer. I like sports okay, especially soccer, but I pass on football and baseball pools. I don't like to lose.

What kind of bet was it? Pamela Yew drove a hard bargain—but from her standpoint I guess I did, too.

I had a painting, a Thomas Eakins, that Ms. Yew coveted in the worst way. I learned about Thomas Eakins as an undergraduate. He was a late nineteenth-century realist who did New England seascapes and renderings of man and nature. My

Eakins, which I inherited from my grandmother, was worth $50,000—I'd had it appraised. Pamela Yew had to expect she'd have to put up something.

All I asked for was a mere weekend of her time. There were details she'd have to see to, of coure, she being the loser and all. I wanted dinner out—at a Japanese restaurant, if possible— *sashimi, sushi, tempura,* pickled vegetables and lots of *sake.* One of those private little rooms where you sit squat-legged would be nice. Later, she might put on one of those little see-through things or something appropriate. She didn't even have to do that; nothing at all would have been fine by me. The next morning, there'd be breakfast in bed: *huevos rancheros* and coffee with cream. That's Saturday morning. The way I saw it, she could take me to see the Sonics that night; I like to drink beer and eat peanuts. After the ball game, I figured we'd sort of slip into bed together and talk about the 24-second limit, the quality of NBA referees, stuff like that.

It'd be easy to choke up and get all romantic with a woman like Pamela Yew.

In any event, a fool and his Eakins are soon parted.

I supported my brains with my shorts. She flew the flag of free women everywhere. What kind of chance did I have?

I knew from the beginning she was quick, knew it from her bearing, knew it from the way her eyes took in everything. Still I underestimated her. She knew I would, of course; she counted on that. It took a while for me to learn she was maybe smarter than I was. Still I made the bet, made it after I knew there was a murderer involved.

It all began when she stepped into my excuse for an office and stood, appraising me casually from under a wide-brimmed hat. In the first place, I have a weakness for women in hats. This was a special woman; the hat made her stunning.

She was in her mid-thirties, tall, maybe five-foot-ten, with auburn hair that fell straight to the middle of her back. Besides the hat, she wore black slacks, a long-sleeved gray blouse, a green tie emblazoned with a rocket blasting off over the word "go," and a maroon blazer with a velvet collar. The blazer had a handkerchief in the breast pocket; a grinning Mickey Mouse

10

was on the handkerchief. He gave a wink and a wave at who-ever noticed him. She wore gold cuff links in the shape of an exclamation point and eyeglasses with lenses as wide as the palm of your hand. The eyes behind the glasses were brown with yellow flecks. They had, I suspected, known streets filled with darting cats and blind corners.

She had a soft face. I noticed a small, thin scar under her left eye. The scar, curiously, didn't detract from her face. She made no attempt to hide it. I wondered how it got there.

She also had, I noticed, a small gold pin on her jacket collar that said, "Ask."

She ran the forefinger of her left hand along the scar as though out of habit. "Well?"

I had a lot of questions but I didn't say anything. I cleared my throat. She gave me a sardonic, knowing smile.

"Mr. John Denson?"

I stood there grinning and feeling foolish. A fly circled above my head. I looked up at the damned thing. "Yes, ma'am. Me and my pardner up there. I've been trying to get him to sell his half of the business to me all afternoon." I gave her handkerchief a wave. "Hiya, Mick!"

She arched one eyebrow, an ability I've always envied, and eyed the nearly empty three-liter jug of red wine on my desk. "I was told you're a private detective, Mr. Denson."

I was embarrassed by the screw-top. With anybody else, I wouldn't have given a damn. "Yes, ma'am, that's what it says there on the door: 'John Denson, Investigations.' I'm a watcher and a listener. Doesn't pay much, but I like hot dogs." I leaned forward for a closer look at the pin on her lapel and gave her my best grin.

She smiled—what novelists sometimes call a thin smile. Since I've never been sure what a thick smile would look like, I'll just call it a smile. Maybe she just didn't have time for people who ate hot dogs. Yes, it was a no-time-for-fools smile. "Are you going to tell me your biography or do you want to make some money?" She handed me a business card: "Pamela Yew, Confidential Investigations, San Francisco." The card gave a Union Street address and telephone number. The name sounded Chinese, but she was obviously an American beauty.

"I go by Pamela. Never Pam. Pams are cheerleaders with boobs that jiggle and bounce up and down when they leap."

I stared at her. "Yours don't?"

She smiled. "What I'm saying, Mr. Denson, is that I keep my feet flat on the ground and my eyes straight ahead. I'm a Pamela, not a Pam."

It was my turn to grin. "Well I'm a John, not a Jack. Jacks piss in sinks and spit on sidewalks. I cry at weddings and sentimental movies. And I've never met a lady detective before."

"A detective, Mr. Denson. But if you insist on qualifying it, then I'm a woman detective. What I really am is an artist, a painter. I'm a detective so I can eat, too. I check forgeries, recover lost art, and appear at auctions to bid for clients who wish to remain anonymous." She looked at the table with the hot plate. "Do you live here, Mr. Denson?"

"No. I have an apartment. I rent this office to make me look legit. I picked this building because it has lawyers and chiropractors. Figured I could use a little class." That drew a raised eyebrow. "I'm a gentleman and a scholar; would you care for some screw-top?"

That's when Pamela Yew spotted my painting. She almost did a double take, but stopped herself. It must have been tough for a woman of her background. There were five young men, all naked, standing around a swimming hole in a lazy river in the country. Two young men had their arms folded, a third crouched, a fourth pointed with his finger at something in the water. Another sat on the bank, watching the young man pointing.

Pamela Yew regarded the painting casually. She didn't say anything for a full fifteen seconds. Then she leaned forward for a closer look.

"I like your painting, Mr. Denson."

"I like it too."

"I have an uncle who I think might like this painting. It isn't for sale, is it?"

"Does your uncle have a spare fifty grand?"

Pamela Yew smiled. "It *is* an original then?"

12

I laughed. "Oh, yes. I've had it appraised."

She look amazed. "What are you doing with it hanging here in your office?"

"I liked the painting before I had any idea who Thomas Eakins was. Thought he was a shortstop. My grandmother gave it to me. Nobody knows how she came by it. I like it. If I sold it I wouldn't have it. I'd blow the money in a year."

She shook her head. "Mr. Denson, you were described to me as a curious person. 'Flake,' I believe was the word used. Do you think that's accurate?"

I grinned. "I don't think there's any doubt about it. As I said, would you care for some screw-top?"

"I don't think so. Mr. Denson . . ."

"John. Does this have anything to do with a missing Botticelli, Renoir, or Van Gogh?"

"No, it has nothing whatever to do with art. It has to do with a sadist, prostitutes, three dead girls, and a fourth maimed for life."

I saw that she had a second scar, running from the corner of her left eye up through her eyebrow. Like the first, you almost had to know it was there to see it. It did not detract from her beauty; it enhanced it: a delicate, tragic flaw on a soft face.

"I'm listening. How could I not want to know about a story like that?"

"Have you ever heard of an organization called Coyote?"

I had, but I wanted to hear her tell about it. "Does it have anything to do with preserving the wilderness?"

"It's an organization of hookers in San Francisco and it's become one of my clients. The media people call it a 'prostitute's' union. Men buy, the women of Coyote sell. An old story. But they earn their money. They have to put up with perverts, sadists, and pimps ready to take ninety cents out of every buck they earn. So they organized."

I looked into the brown eyes. "How is it that Coyote became your client. Do they paint abstracts? Nudes maybe?"

Pamela Yew grinned. "The younger sister of an artist friend of mine is a call girl. She works lawyers and businessmen in conventions at classy hotels. She is said to be one of the most

13

beautiful call girls in the Bay area. Coyote needed help; she steered the business my way."

I helped myself to a piece of raw broccoli from a paper bag and offered her some. She shook her head no.

"The sisters, as they call themselves, pay me to do something that has to be done."

"And that is?"

"See that justice is done, Mr. Denson. Your conversations with clients are privileged in this state, are they not?"

"They are indeed, Ms. Yew. Whatever you say stays with me. But like I said, I'm a watcher and a listener. What I see is a woman who's had the left side of her face cut. And what I hear is the kind of story that leads to creepy places. As they say, I gotta know the truth, the whole truth, and nothing but— or we don't do business."

She looked straight at me with those brown eyes and ran her finger along the lower scar again. "I flipped a Saab just south of Modesto, Mr. Denson. Killed my sister."

That shut me up, but I didn't believe her. "I'm sorry," I said.

"No need. As for creepy places, I can handle myself, thank you." She reached into her handbag and withdrew a .38 caliber Beretta.

"Well, I don't carry a piece, Pamela. Now you take that fly there; I'll squash the little sucker sooner or later. And in a week or so I'll be out there in the wind and snow waiting for geese. But I don't shoot people. I did that once. No more."

Pamela Yew didn't budge from her chair. I was glad she didn't, really. "Are you willing to listen to my story, Mr. Denson? I was simply trying to make it clear that I can take care of myself."

"Sure, I'll listen to anybody."

"Then maybe I'll have some of your screw-top after all. But only a little, I'm what is known as a cheap drunk."

I poured her half a glass of Mr. Gallo's best. "By all means, talk then."

"I'm told it's the worst when you're sixteen years old and out there on the street by yourself, maybe supporting a pimp

14

in a Lincoln Continental. The girl who got me this job was a fast learner and beautiful. She wanted money and a lot of it. When you look like she does, the Johns make appointments. She gets middle-aged Johns who have never seen a woman like her naked, much less crawl into bed with her. She says they're more in awe than anything else. They want relief and a few minutes next to a beautiful woman just to know what it's like. But she's able to draw the line at the nutty stuff; she can afford to. But some of the girls have real problems; they go for the rough stuff. One of them gets beaten half to death, the cops say they're asking for it. One of them gets murdered, the cops ask questions for a couple of days and call it quits. Where's the justice in that, Mr. Denson?"

"John's my name. Beautiful woman's just like a plain one—sometimes not as good."

"John, then. Where's the justice?" She waited; I said nothing. "In 1977 a pimp named Jay Hamarr worked call girls out of the best hotels in the city. They were maybe the most beautiful call girls in town—everybody seems to agree on that. Hamarr charged the highest rates. The Johns paid. Hamarr's kind of customers had money; they were entertainers, doctors, lawyers, business executives of one sort or another, politicians, and so on. They demanded absolute assurance that their pleasure would be held confidential. Hamarr guaranteed that. He wanted to run a special kind of business. He found the pimp who had the best-looking girls in town, a fairly decent guy named Roger Gaines, and took over. Gaines just disappeared one day. We don't know what happened to him."

"Do you think Hamarr killed him?"

Pamela Yew smiled. "That's probably what happened. We'll never be able to prove it. Anyway, two years later a gorgeous girl with the down-home name of Sarah Milne was indiscreet about one of her famous clients, an entertainer." Pamela took a photograph out of her handbag and laid it on the table.

Sarah Milne was indeed lovely. "Beautiful girl," I said.

Pamela left the picture on the table. "Jay Hamarr gathered a few of his girls together in his penthouse. As a lesson to what happens to whores who talk too much, he tied Sarah's hands behind her back and beat her with brass knuckles." Pamela dipped into her purse for a second picture. She laid it on the table.

It almost made me vomit. I turned it over quickly. "Sarah Milne?"

"She either can't speak or won't. She was blinded. She lost the use of her right arm and right leg. Plastic surgeons say they could make her face look roughly human with enough time and money. But what's the use? She's in an institution, cared for by the state of California. She's incontinent and has to be fed by an attendant. She sits all day and stares at a wall. Brain damage, the doctors say." Pamela looked at me again.

"I still don't shoot people."

"I'm not asking you to. Let me finish my story." She dipped into her handbag a third time. She withdrew a handful of photographs and fanned them out on the table like a deck of cards. They were various pictures of three young women, gorgeous women who could have been actresses or models. "These were the girls who watched Jay Hamarr destroy Sarah Milne. This happened four years ago. In two years these girls were all dead. Two of them had their throats cut; one of them was blown in half by a .44 Magnum."

"Why would he destroy a profitable business?"

"Because the ladies of Coyote were pressuring the girls to turn him into the cops for what he had done to Sarah Milne. He was scared."

"And the cops?"

"There are cops we can talk to. They say Hamarr murdered them one by one, in cold blood, but they can't prove it."

"Where is this Hamarr now?"

Pamela looked at me, closed her eyes and said nothing for fully thirty seconds. "Would you look at these pictures again?"

I looked.

"They were murdered. By one man." Pamela Yew's face tightened. There were tears in her eyes but she willed them not to come.

I poured us some more screw-top to give her a break and leaned back on the rear two legs of my chair. There were a whole lot of questions I wanted to ask. "What's he look like?"

Pamela rubbed her eyes with the back of her hand. "We don't know what he looks like, Mr. Denson. We have no idea." She turned slightly and the scars around her eye disappeared; they were visible only when the light was bright and hard on her face.

"What? You're telling me he maimed one girl and murdered three more and you don't know what he looks like?"

"The cops don't even know his name; I found that out on my own. Hamarr believed in keeping his business confidential and himself anonymous. The girls who knew what he looked like are all dead. You asked me where he lives. We think we know that."

I leaned forward. "Where?"

Pamela Yew smiled. "In a small town on the Oregon side of the Columbia River."

I put all four legs of my chair on the floor. "In a small town on the Oregon side?"

"That's right," she said.

"East or west of Portland?"

"East."

"How far east?"

She shrugged her shoulders. "Oh, a couple of hundred miles, maybe. Something like that."

"Cayuse," I said.

"I didn't say that."

"It's why you're here, isn't it." Cayuse, Oregon, was my home town.

"If he was in Spokane I wouldn't be here, Mr. Denson."

"If you don't know what he looks like, how could you possibly know where he lives? I gotta admit this one's by me."

"We don't for sure. It was one of those one-in-a-million strokes of luck. One of the Coyote women is from Pendleton, where they have the Roundup. She was going home to visit her parents who think she works as a hostess in a San Francisco hotel lounge. She took a plane to Portland and was going the rest of the way on the Greyhound. The bus broke down in

17

Cayuse. She had three hours to pass so she went to a local bar."

"Sandy Johnson's. He's a friend of mine."

"That's the place. She was at the bar having a drink when she heard a guy threaten his wife. He said, 'I had a whore in San Francisco cross me like you just did. Beat her till she was blind and couldn't talk.' "

"San Francisco? He said San Francisco?"

"That's what he said."

"Not much to go on. Maybe he wasn't a pimp at all. Maybe he was a sadistic John. How do you know?"

"We don't. We've been after him for two years. We check everything, Mr. Denson, and this tip's better than most, I can assure you."

"Maybe he was just mouthing off."

"That's possible. We'll find out, one way or the other."

"So what did your friend do?"

"She finished her drink, found a phone, and called a girl-friend in San Francisco. We've had these kinds of leads before and nothing happened. This time I think we've got him. I've got a feeling."

I shook my head. "You've got a feeling?"

"A good one. We need you to help us check it out."

I leaned back again on the rear legs of the chair. "Me? Why do you want me?"

Pamela Yew took a small sip of wine. "We want you because you're from Cayuse, John Denson, home town boy."

"How did you find that out?"

"We were wondering how we were going to get into Cayuse unobtrusively to do a little checking when one of our gals here in Seattle read a feature article about you in a newspaper here."

The fly returned. It made a half-hearted pass at my wine glass but thought better of it.

"We have solid contacts in all major cities, Mr. Denson. If Jay Hamarr showed up as a pimp in Times Square we'd know about it. The same is true of Detroit, of Chicago, of Los Angeles, of almost all American cities. The odds are he'd try

18

to establish a setup similar to the one he had in San Francisco. That one worked for him. It made him a lot of money."

"And?"

"Nothing. We've checked everywhere. We've got Italians in New York working for us, Irishmen in Boston, black men in the District, Koreans in Honolulu, you name it. Nothing. Even if he switched rackets we'd know about it. Not a word. He vanished."

"An underworld APB. Leaving you to conclude what?"

Pamela Yew smiled. "Leaving us to conclude he's scared witless that some day a sweet young thing with bedroom eyes is going to give him a smile one second and a blade between his ribs the next. What would you do under those circumstances, Mr. Denson?"

I thought about that. "I believe I just might stay away from places like The Block in Baltimore and the Combat Zone in Boston. I might spring for a fried chicken outlet in Cheyenne and keep my eyes wide, wide open."

"That's what we think too. He knows he has to watch for a woman, not a man, right?"

"Makes sense."

"If Jay Hamarr does live in Cayuse, he very likely settled there for his own protection—to rob us of the element of surprise. A strange woman can't be anonymous in a town that small."

"So?"

"So we need cover, Mr. Denson. We want you to take me home to Cayuse and introduce me to your mother and your friends as your lady."

The idea of me introducing Pamela Yew as my lady struck me as funny. I erupted into a raucous guffaw.

"What's the matter, Mr. Denson? Aren't I good looking enough for you? Or maybe you like women to be shy and act dumb. I could try that but it wouldn't be easy."

"My heavens, it's certainly not that," I said, wiping tears from my eyes with the back of my hand. "It's just that if I go back to that place with a woman like you on my arm those poor people won't know what to think. My mother will con-

19

clude we're about to be married. My old man will stare in randy admiration. He'll think that I've finally amounted to something. My friends will be sick with envy. They'll want to know what's wrong with you. There'll have to be something wrong. Epilepsy, maybe? What's it worth to you?"

"Maybe you should pay me!"

"Oh, no!"

"How about one hundred dollars a day? All you have to do is stand around looking gooney-eyed and smitten. Tell them I'm an artist. I'll look at you as though you're the conquering stud, great he-man and all that." That last part struck her as funny and she started laughing again. Pamela Yew knew how to laugh; I'll give her that.

"Do we shake on it or what?"

"No or-whats, Mr. Denson. This is business. We shake on it."

We shook.

"Listen," I said. "We'll have to share the same bed, you know; truly beloveds these days always do it. Especially at our age."

Pamela shook her head. "You're right about the one-bed business; we need that for cover. But this is strictly platonic, Mr. Denson. I'm not interested in romance with you. I'm not interested in sex. I do just fine by myself. I'm only interested in bringing Jay Hamarr to justice."

"Ah well." I shrugged. "Here's to truly beloveds." I held up my glass for a toast.

"I have my own life, Mr. Denson; it does not include men. I have my reasons. They're mine. I insist on my privacy."

"I understand," I said. It wasn't the brightest statement.

She shook her head. "No, you don't. You don't understand and I'll thank you not to try. I'm paying you well to do a job. Please do that and no more."

I poured myself some more wine. "Even if you go to Cayuse as my lady you can't go charging around asking questions yourself. You know that, don't you?"

"Meaning what, Mr. Denson?"

"Meaning in places like Cayuse, people are a trifle backward

20

by feminist standards. The little lady in Cayuse stays home with Mom while the menfolk do the work."

Pamela Yew did not like that. "You're saying I stay home with your parents."

"While I find the truth about your man Hamarr, if that's who he is."

She thought about that. "I do my own work, Mr. Denson."

"Here, in Seattle, yes. There, no."

"So what are you proposing?"

"Why don't you just hire me to check Hamarr out and report back."

"I'll go along."

"You'll go along?"

"Yes. If I have to play the little woman I'll play the little woman but I go."

I shrugged. "Fine by me. Pamela, my love, when would you like to begin this platonic romance of ours, conceived as it is in cynicism and monetary gain?"

Pamela Yew considered that. She straightened her tie with the rocket on it and traced a pattern on the velvet of her collar. "How about tomorrow?" She turned her attention again to my Eakins.

"You'll have to go easy on the luggage. Not much room in my Fiat."

Pamela looked surprised. "I thought we'd take my car!"

"Oh?"

"I drive a BMW. Lots of room. If you're going to wow your pals you may as well go all the way."

My refrigerator went into one of its periodic fits of clattering. I stood up. "Why hell yes, Ms. Yew, we'll drive your BMW. Beautiful woman. Beautiful car. I'll wear my English touring cap and maybe a yellow ascot with black polka dots."

Pamela Yew smiled. "Do you have the touring cap?"

"I've got all kinds of caps: Irish country hats, a grouser, a Panama; you name it."

"How about the ascot?"

"Don't have an ascot."

"I'll bring the ascot and the BMW." Pamela Yew stood up to leave.

"What do you say we meet here at nine in the morning?"

"Done," she said. She opened the door, looked back and shook her head sadly. "God, what have I done?"

"Lucky girl."

She looked to the heavens for help. None was forthcoming. She was stuck with me.

Two

AT NINE O'CLOCK ON THE nose Pamela Yew rapped twice on my office door. I opened it and there she stood with a pale green ascot in one hand and a tweedy herringbone jacket in the other. The jacket had leather patches on the elbows. "Off with the corduroy and on with this." She grinned. "I don't like to decorate my arm with shabby-looking males. Bad for the reputation."

It fit perfectly. I was bewildered. "How did you know my size?"

"I didn't. That jacket belonged to my late husband, a professor. He ran off with a giggler and left this behind."

"Your late husband? He's dead, then."

"No, he was always late. He was never on time, drove me nuts. It even fits you in the sleeves."

I lugged my worn leather traveling bag after her. We packed it into the trunk of her silver BMW. It was cold and a biting wind whipped across the city. She slipped behind the wheel; I took the passenger side.

"It's snowing in the pass; we'd better go by Portland and up the gorge," she said. She found the nearest exit to I-5 and the BMW purred south Pamela beat fifty-five by maybe twenty. When it began snowing at Tacoma she only slowed five. I listened to pop music on the tape deck, watched the snow settle lightly on the fields and evergreens. We were more than four hours from Portland because of the snow when we switched. I took the BMW up I-80 east to Cayuse, Oregon, pop. 800, and a rendezvous with a pimp named Jay Hamarr.

At Cascade Locks and Bonneville Dam, where the Columbia cuts through the Cascade chain, the snow really began to come. The traffic merged into one lane that was no more than parallel trails in the accumulating snow. The wind was coming at thirty-five, maybe forty miles an hour; visibility was no more than a car length. I idled the BMW along behind a Ford van. We inched into the storm that twisted and whipped down the gorge. It was going to be a long ride to Cayuse.

"Well, what the hell? What I'm wondering, Ms. Yew, is what you're holding back from me with this prostitute story of yours?"

She raised an eyebrow. "Holding back?"

"I've been in this business awhile. I get a feeling sometimes. I get a feeling I listen to it. Always. I got a feeling now. It says you haven't told me everything I should know."

Pamela Yew popped some jazz into her tape deck. "I too have been in this business awhile, Mr. Denson. I can't imagine anything you need to know that I haven't already told you."

I shrugged. The Ford van slowed ahead of me; I braked. The BMW fishtailed in the snow.

We were stalled for two hours in the snow between Hood River and The Dalles. It took us ten hours to make what should have been a three-and-a-half-hour drive from Portland to Cayuse. It was eleven p.m. when we neared my parents' small farm a mile from town. I stopped the BMW in front of the house next door.

"We're here," I said and poked Pamela, who had fallen asleep against the door.

"What?" She looked outside at the snow coming down.

"Actually, we're next door, but I've got to see a man a few minutes before I go home."

"I don't understand." She looked confused.

"I hope to go goose hunting in the morning. Be back in a minute."

I gave a few loud raps on Sullivan's door. He opened it, wondering who would be knocking at eleven o'clock in a snowstorm.

"Denson, you fucker."

I kicked the snow from my shoes and stepped inside. It was warm. I could hear the television set in the living room. "Bitch of a night."

"I've got some hot water on. Would you like a little snort of Uncle Jim?" Without waiting for my answer he poured four fingers of Jim Beam into a cup and added a touch of water. "James Bond's on the tube."

"Can't stay long, got a gal in the car."

Sullivan looked disappointed. "A gal. She care if you shoot geese?"

"Think they'll be flying?"

"We'll kill 'em in this weather."

"You're on," I said. I raised my whiskey for a toast.

Sullivan looked outside at the BMW and whistled. "Jesus, you own that?"

"My gal's," I said. I couldn't wait for him to repeat the question.

"Your lady owns that car?" Sullivan assumed I was going to get married; I knew he would. He looked like he'd been hit between the eyes with a two-by-four. "You're going to get married."

I shrugged. "I didn't say that."

That confirmed it in his mind. "To a gal who owns a car like that!" He leaned closer to the window.

"You should see the lady."

Sullivan peered out into the snow and blackness of the night. "Bring her in, for Christ's sakes."

I loved it. "Back in a minute. Can't stay long, though." I went back into the snow and rapped on the window on Pamela's side. The window came down a crack.

"What do you want?" She looked exhausted.

I grinned. "I want you to meet a friend."

She looked at me like I was crazy. "At this time of night?"

"Sullivan and I are going goose hunting in the morning. You have to meet him. That's the way things are done in this part of the country. He'll offer you whiskey straight up."

"Do I have to drink it?"

"If you don't he'll wonder how it was I ever asked you out twice. We have to do this thing right if we do it at all."

"You bastard." She managed a smile in spite of it all. Not a bad woman. She got out and trailed after me through the snow.

She stepped through the door and flipped her long brown hair to one side. Sullivan had a drink ready for her but just stared stupidly.

"Jim Sullivan, I'd like you to meet my lady, Pamela Yew."

"Pamela, not Pam," she said. She accepted his drink.

"Wife's gone to bed or I'd bring her out." Sullivan stared at Pamela like she was some kind of exotic bird. I wondered if he was still breathing.

"How long have you known John?"

Pamela smiled. "Oh, what, John? Five months now."

"Something like that. Sullivan and I went to high school together, Pamela."

"Oh!" she said, as though she cared.

I'd put her through enough. "What time in the morning, Sullivan?"

John Denson with a gorgeous brunette in a silver BMW. Sullivan was overwhelmed. He snapped out of his trance. "Why don't you see if you can con your old man's pickup. My jeep's on the blink. Say four thirty so we can spread the dekes before light."

I slipped my hand around Pamela's waist, rested it on her hip and gave her a little squeeze. I surprised her but she managed not to flinch. She nuzzled her face against the side of my face.

"Jerk," she whispered in my ear.

I gave her a big hug for that endearment. Sullivan looked embarrassed. "See you in the morning, Jim," I said.

26

Pamela glared at me after we had settled into the front seat of the BMW but didn't say anything.

"More of the same coming up, Ms. Yew. My mother thinks I'm the Second Coming. You'll have to display proper affection."

Pamela smiled. "My time will come."

"You'll have to sleep on a freezing porch tonight, you know."

"What?"

"My folks have a small house, only one bedroom. I sleep on the porch. It has a double bed with an electric blanket and a portable heater that sometimes works."

"Sometimes?"

"Sometimes not, but the blanket works."

"You didn't tell me that."

"Pamela, when you ask a man to take you home with him, you take the bad with the good."

"Where's the good?"

"Quiet now." I parked the car and we went inside to meet my mother. She was eating walnuts and watching the same James Bond movie as Jim Sullivan. My father had apparently gone to bed.

"Why, hello, John. I didn't know you were coming up." She was so used to seeing me alone it took her a moment to realize I had a woman with me.

Pamela Yew watched me with a slight grin. I was slightly embarrassed by my mother and Pamela knew it.

"Mom, I'd like you to meet Pamela Yew. Pamela and I are good friends."

"Pleased to meet you, Mrs. Denson."

"I was just watching James Bond on TV," my mother said. Poor woman. She didn't know what to say. "I don't know where we're going to put everybody," she said and looked about her frantically.

"Relax, mom, Pamela and I aren't nineteen years old, if you get my drift."

"Oh!" She looked quickly at Pamela. "You're not going to take her out on that porch, are you? She'll freeze." Apparently it didn't make any difference if I froze.

"The blanket still works, I take it. We'll generate any extra heat ourselves."

With that, Pamela Yew slipped her arm around my waist and gave me a lovely kiss. My mother beamed. An affectionate girl with taste. She likes my John.

"That was for your mother. It's as close as you're ever going to get, bub," Pamela said as I retrieved our luggage from the BMW. She followed me to the porch. "Good God!" she said when she stepped through the door. The porch was screened in but there was no glass. It was like sleeping outside.

I turned on the electric blanket. I tried the heater on the floor but it didn't work. I undressed quickly, threw my clothes on a chair at the foot of the bed and leaped bravely under the covers. My spine stiffened from the cold but I gritted my teeth and took it. Pamela undressed with her back to me. I watched her silhouette slip into pajamas in the darkness. She slipped a hand hesitantly under the covers.

"Oh, God!"

"Yes?"

"How can you take it?"

"Not easy, Ms. Yew. Body heat's the best bet."

She eased under the covers without saying anything. I felt her body stiffen on the other side of the bed. She sucked in a lungful of air. "Good Christ!" she breathed.

"Hang tough, it'll be okay once the blanket gets warmed up."

We lay there in silence as we waited for the Sears Roebuck electric blanket to give us some relief. I moved my hand over and rested it on her thigh.

"Your hand is on my thigh, Mr. Denson."

"Your thigh?"

"Yes, that's what it is. Connects with my knee at the lower end, my hip at the upper."

"I like it a lot," I said and gave the thigh a little squeeze.

"So do I, but you'll please remove your goddam hand."

I removed it. "I only use the hand for warmups. I don't know what kind of men you've been hanging out with."

"A paw artist."

"I don't know about that." I tried to sound hurt. "Dr. Comfort says the light touch is the best touch."

"God!" She sounded disgusted.

"Ah well."

"How is it you're going to know when to get up to hunt with your friend Sullivan?"

"Clock inside my head. Time comes, I'll be up and gone. I'm sorry to have to leave you alone with my mother. We'll be stopping off at Sandy Johnson's on our way back from the fields tomorrow. I'll see if I can't learn something about your man Jay Hamarr."

"Thank you."

"Wouldn't it be lovely if this were real between us."

"It's hard to imagine, Mr. Denson," she said and fell silent. We went to sleep.

Three

I SLIPPED OUT OF BED without waking Pamela. I got my hunting clothes out of the battered trunk where they were stored. They were ice cold. I watched Pamela Yew sleeping as I struggled into long johns and two pairs of pants. Her face was soft and trusting in sleep. I finished lacing my boots and touched her hair lightly with my hand before I opened the door to go, shotgun in hand.

"You be careful now, Mr. Denson."

"I thought you were asleep."

"I know. You look ridiculous in long johns."

"I'll be careful." I closed the door. The snow was a foot deep and still coming down. My old man's truck turned over the first grunt. I eased down the road to Jim Sullivan's.

Sullivan was making coffee when I tapped on the door. He padded around the kitchen in heavy wool socks that were too large for him and stretched out of shape. He motioned with a finger to his lips that I should whisper.

"Think they'll be flying?" I asked. I leaned against a counter and watched Sullivan's socks as he moved about the floor. Sullivan pulled at the suspenders of his trousers. He didn't say anything.

"Where in the hell did a jerk like you meet a woman like that?" he whispered.

"She's a painter. I met her at an art reception."

Sullivan shook his head.

I listened for the geese outside on the Columbia River. Sometimes you could hear them rustling on the banks. At least you could when I was a kid. The river was a game reserve but the geese wouldn't stay there. They never had. They would move south at daybreak. They would gabble and squawk for about thirty minutes in the darkness. Then they would go. It was in their blood. It was the same every winter.

Sullivan must have left his boots in the garage because they were frozen stiff. He muttered something about his wife and struggled with the brittle laces.

"Goddamned thermos." Sullivan had screwed the lid on crooked. He unscrewed it and tried again; it slipped into place. "Let's move butts," he said.

The north wind blew snow across the whiteness. I turned my back to the wind and swung two gunnysacks of Sullivan's decoys into the back of the pickup. The geese were beginning to stir on the river.

"Just listen to them suckers," Sullivan said. "This wind'll keep 'em real low."

The snow twisted and billowed in front of the pickup's yellow headlights.

"Fucking cold." Sullivan peered out into the darkness and coughed once. He muffled the cough with the back of his hand. He had a small bird tattooed on his wrist. He turned the radio into some country and western music and settled back on the cold plastic seat covers to sing along with Hank Williams. The old truck had a good heater, a floor model that glowed orange in the cab. It had an old-fashioned fan with brittle rubber blades that went whump, whump, whump. It was just a mile to Cayuse and another five to the fields.

There was a glow in the east when I parked the truck in a grove of locust trees. We started down a frozen irrigation ditch by foot. The heavy gunnysacks of decoys cut into our shoulders. My feet were already cold inside my boots. After a hundred yards, Sullivan slowed up. I watched the close-cropped hair on the back of his neck.

"I think I heard something," he whispered.

"So did I," I said. "But I don't think it was geese." I watched his eyes.

"I'm not sure," said Sullivan.

"Neither am I." I was aware of my heart beating. Maybe the sound was a dog barking at some farm house. I shifted the sacks of decoys from one shoulder to the other.

Sullivan set the decoys while I piled tumbleweeds over a large hole where the ditch had washed out in the summer. Sullivan was careful that each decoy was set just so, facing the wind mostly. Some people had a knack for laying a spread. It's something you're born with. Sullivan was one of those. Only when he was satisfied were we ready. We settled in under the frozen tumbleweeds for the wait.

"Remember, when they come don't look up until they're right on top of us."

"You give the word," I said. Already the cold had worked its way through the soles of my boots. I was wondering why I hadn't stayed in bed listening to Pamela Yew breathing on the other side. I'd missed out on some good teasing. She'd have to get up eventually and there I'd be. In another hour my toes would be miserable stubs. I tried to keep them moving. Sullivan poured us each a cup of coffee from his thermos.

"Those decoys look good in the snow," I said.

"We could use a few more, make a better spread. Geese are like people; they need companionship. They go for numbers."

I began shifting my weight from foot to foot to keep the blood moving.

"What if they don't come today?" I asked.

Sullivan looked at me like I was a fool. He wiped his nose with the back of his hand. "Geese gotta eat, don't they? They get cold and restless out there on the river. The reservoir's no better."

I stared out into the snow. I wanted to take off my boots to massage my toes but I knew that would be a mistake with Sullivan around. Sullivan could endure anything. Besides, I knew my feet would be even colder when I got my boots back on.

"Geese are like women, Denson. They can't do it differently. After a while you get to know how they think. What else are they going to do? On a day like this they'll take chances." Sullivan looked at me over his plastic coffee cup and grinned. "They'll come, Denson." He laughed at my ignorance.

Geese are like women. I watched Sullivan dig at his ear, then look at his finger. I thought of Pamela Yew.

"What if they get tired of being shot at and decide to do it all differently?" I asked.

Sullivan shook his head at my ignorance.

We had been hunkered under the tumbleweeds for more than an hour when we first heard geese. The wind had eased some; the snow was heavier.

"Maybe we've got too much of a good thing. Maybe they can't see the decoys," I said.

"They'll come. They'll see those cardboard geese out there and think they've got a good thing. They're always lonely, geese are, you can tell by listening to them. They're hungry sitting out there on the river all night staring at shadows of willow trees. They can see for miles but they're still suckers if you know how to lay a spread. We've got the shotguns; they've got to eat."

Sullivan peered out into the snow and grayness. I concentrated on kneading my feet through the rubber boots. When your feet are cold you're cold all over.

We heard two more flights pass unseen in the snow before Sullivan trotted out onto the field to adjust the decoys.

"We'll be seeing some action," he said when he came back. Sullivan knew how to wait. He took the plug out of his shotgun so he could get five shots instead of the legal three. "No way a game warden could get to us without being seen."

I thought I heard something and started to paw an opening in the tumbleweeds with my hands.

"Don't look up!" Sullivan whispered harshly. "Don't look up! What is it?"

I didn't answer. I shifted my weight slightly. Sullivan didn't like people messing with the cover. My left foot had gone to sleep.

"We'll get plenty of warning when they get really close. We'll be able to hear their wings," Sullivan whispered. He was stopped by the smallest of sounds in the distance.

I held my breath so I could hear better. Blood thumped in my ears. But he had heard something. Yes, there it was again. Again. Then four, five. I realized Sullivan was right: the geese did sound lonely. They were looking for others of their kind. They seemed certain of sanctuary in spite of the snow and danger.

I stared at my feet and listened as the cries grew nearer. The geese circled warily to our left. They had spotted the decoys. I looked at Sullivan; his eyes stared unseeing at the frozen mud wall of the ditch. He was calculating time and distance. When at last Sullivan blinked, turtle-like, I eased off the safety of my shotgun.

Then came the telling sound of wings, an odd buzzing that said the geese were closer, closer . . .

"Now!" yelled Sullivan and he swung his shotgun skyward in one smooth motion.

He took three quick shots. The geese swept upward with startling quickness before I could react. I hesitated. I couldn't help it.

I pulled down on a goose that wasn't really a goose. It was a dream played in fast motion. I fired once. Then again. The geese were out of range when I fired a third time. The last shot was futile. I knew that when I pulled the trigger.

Sullivan was already sprinting through the snow.

"You winged one," he shouted back over his shoulder.

My hands were trembling. I was aware of the lush softness of the falling snow. I had lost something I once had.

"You can forget him," Sullivan yelled.

I saw the lone goose losing altitude, struggling to overcome a crippled wing. It had been fooled by paper geese. It was bleeding because of it. It was a dark gray spot that became smaller and smaller until it disappeared over the dim locust trees across the fields.

34

Beyond the trees there was a gravel road and beyond the road some corn stubble. I felt the cold metal of my shotgun. I remembered clearly the hollow thump of my last shot. The wind had stopped, I realized. It was as if my senses hadn't been working all morning. I could smell now. I could see. The feeling was exhilarating. The snow was falling more heavily; the horizons closed in. The river was a world away and the towns and the farms. There was just the soft snow coming down. The cold. Sullivan. The crippled goose out there alone in the snow.

Sullivan had four big honkers by the feet when he returned. "Beautiful, huh?" He held them up. "This is when you get geese, weather like this."

In another hour the geese stopped flying; we packed our gear and headed back. When we were loading the truck Sullivan discovered that one of his geese had an aluminum band around its foot. It was the first time either of us had shot a bird that had been tagged.

We agreed to have breakfast at Sandy Johnson's, followed by a drink in his bar. A red and green neon sign flickered and blinked outside. From my seat in a wooden booth, I could see the cemetery across the street. The snow, which had fallen off, picked up again and rushed violently against the window panes. I wondered how old Sullivan's goose was and what he had been through. Sullivan said he would mail the tag to the federal people.

It took me a moment to recognize the waitress. She had a plastic name tag on the front of her nylon uniform. The tag said she was Linda. She was Linda Armstrong. The Armstrong sisters, Linda and an identical twin named Leanne, were once neighbors of mine. I used to hunt geese with their father. But he was a far different hunting companion than Sullivan. His name was Roger and he didn't belong in Cayuse. Everybody knew that without knowing quite why. He was an engineer of some kind at a power station but he never talked about his work and apparently wasn't especially interested in it.

I wish I had asked him what he had done before Cayuse. It was one of those unasked questions I've always regretted.

I was just a kid then; the only things I thought about were sex and my inability to hit a jump shot with somebody waving his hand in my face. Roger was understanding about the sex part but said I was wasting my time worrying about jump shots. One day in a duck blind he started to tell me about Hemingway's Nick Adams short stories but stopped with a smile when he discovered I didn't know what he was talking about. Every weekend in the fall and early winter we sat waiting over his decoys for the ducks or geese to come. He didn't care if I didn't know the difference between Nick Adams and Bob Cousy. He found out I liked limericks; he must have known a hundred of them about girls from Nantucket and men from Khartoum and elsewhere.

One summer day with my questions still unasked, Roger Armstrong and his wife were killed in a traffic accident. Their Ford was sideswiped by a wheat truck, with the brakes out. I was stunned. A lone woman, Roger's sister, arrived from California to attend the funeral and take the girls. After the burial I gave the sister a piece of paper with my name and my parents' address.

"Please write to me at this address if you ever need help with the girls," I said. "Their father was my friend."

She must have thought I was crazy, a seventeen-year-old with pimples. "Are you the young man who went hunting with Roger?"

"Yes, ma'am."

"Thank you for your concern, John." She put the piece of paper in her purse and was gone with the twins. Of course she didn't understand. She couldn't have. But it was real to me.

That was years ago. Now the twins were back, at least one. I assumed the other would be somewhere in the area. That's the way it is with twins.

Linda had her father's hazel eyes. She was slender and small breasted. She was cute in the fresh, high-spirited manner associated with cheerleaders and models in Pepsi-Cola ads. Women who are beautiful are cosmopolitan and self-assured with classic features and long legs. Linda Hammond was vulnerable, hesitant in the manner of a woman accustomed to watching for cues from men.

It was hard for me to look her in the eyes without feeling exposed. She knew that and was flattered.

I remembered one of the last times I saw her. She and Leanne couldn't have been more than eight years old. It was Halloween night. They came dressed in identical princess outfits.

"Are you two looking for a handsome prince tonight?" my mother had asked.

"I don't know," one of them said from behind her mask.

"Two handsome princes," I said. I embarrassed them. Their small feet danced nervously.

"Well, maybe just one then," my mother said quickly.

Their small shoulders shrugged. They took their candy and ran to the car where their mother waited.

"Hey, do you remember me?" I asked when she poured my coffee.

"I sure do, you're John Denson. You used to hunt geese with my father. You drove your car into our irrigation ditch one night when you were drunk."

"He hasn't changed much." Sullivan grinned.

"Hunting has never been the same since your father. No offense, Sullivan."

"Is it true that you're a detective in Seattle?" she asked me.

"If you ever have need of a detective in Seattle just give me a ring; I'll give you a rate."

Sullivan stared at her rear end as she walked back to the counter. "Bet that'd be a hell of a piece," he said. "Too bad she's married."

I felt like dumping his coffee on his head. "Who's her husband?"

Sullivan shook his head. "A guy named Jerry Hammond. If you hang around Sandy Johnson's a few afternoons you'll meet him. He sits around drinking boilermakers and talking about himself. Struts around in fancy cowboy boots. Busted a guy up a couple Fridays ago."

"What does he do?"

37

"What does he do? Not much of anything I can see. Told me he was 'retired' but that's crap. Said he was in the real estate business in California. He just walked in here about a year ago and ordered himself a boilermaker. Been here damned every afternoon since except when he takes off."

"What do you mean takes off?"

"I mean he just takes off, disappears. He'll be gone two, three weeks at a time then one day he'll just stroll in here with his cowboy boots and order a boilermaker like nothing ever happened."

"Does he tell you where he goes?"

Sullivan laughed. "You don't know Hammond. I'll bet his wife doesn't even know."

"What do you think he does?"

"I think he's got some kind of scam going, in Portland, maybe, or Seattle."

I put some more cream in my coffee. "What kind of scam? I thought he spent all the time talking about himself."

Sullivan took a long, crass drag on his plugged sinuses. "Doesn't talk about anything except California and how many guys he's busted up and how many women he's laid. I believe him, Denson. I've seen him in action and I sure as hell wouldn't tangle with him."

"Hammond. His name is Hammond?"

"That's right, Jerry Hammond."

"How about her sister?"

Sullivan took a sip of coffee and watched Linda put bakery pies in a glass display case with a "Home Baked Pies" card on top. "She was here a few weeks ago, I think, but she lives in Seattle or somewhere."

After breakfast Sullivan and I adjourned to Sandy Johnson's bar. There was a football game on the television set nestled in among gin bottles; it was the first of that day's bowl offerings.

Sullivan ordered whiskey straight up with a water chase. He wanted to brag about his geese and talk about the snow. I had a Bloody Mary and stared at the awful paintings of mountain lakes on the walls. I'd have to bring Pamela Yew to Sandy's so she could really know what bar art was all about. I always

38

went to see Sandy when I got in from Seattle, which was only once or twice a year. He was my only relief from the boredom of Cayuse.

"Dr. Livingstone, I presume," said Sandy.

Sullivan looked at him like he was a bit odd. Jim didn't know Dr. Livingstone from Dr. Pepper. He only wanted to talk about his geese. "Got *four* beauties. Denson here winged one in the first bunch but couldn't hit his ass after that."

"It's been a while between shooting," I said. The Bloody Mary was good.

"You have to come down on 'em and squeeze 'em off, John."

Sandy tried to rescue me. "I don't imagine you get much shooting up in Seattle."

"Nerve, Denson. You have to want geese."

I shrugged. Sullivan kept on talking. "Tomorrow will be good, too. Anytime you get snow like this with a wind the geese have to come down low to find the fields."

"Fellow in earlier said he got five," said Sandy. He watched Sullivan's face. So did I.

"Another Uncle Jim," said Sullivan. He didn't like anybody else getting five on the same day he'd hit for four.

Sandy poured the drink and took his time returning the bottle to its place. Nobody said anything. I sipped my Bloody Mary. Sandy busied himself cleaning up behind the bar.

Sullivan didn't want to ask the question but he couldn't stop. "Who was it got the five?" He dug at the crotch of his pants and tried to look casual.

"Fred Campbell. In here with his cousin, that big redhead who works for a potato outfit. Honch of some kind. They were out by the reservoir like you."

"They both get birds?"

"The redhead got one."

"Get him and Denson together and you'd have some real shooting." Sullivan laughed.

I wanted to get away from the subject of Campbell's five but Sullivan wasn't having any part of it; he got downright vicious.

"Denson showed up on my doorstep last night with a gorgeous brunette in tow. Broad owns a fancy BMW and looks like a million bucks. Says he's gonna marry her. Man can't shoot a gun any better than he can is gonna have a helluva time with a woman like that." The combination of whiskey and Campbell's five was just too much.

Sandy grinned and shook my hand over the bar. "Congratulations, John, bring her in and I'll buy her a drink."

"I didn't say I was going to marry her. Jim's got that wrong."

Sullivan laughed. "Sure, they always say that. I'll tell you, Sandy, that brunette's too much woman for Denson."

What could I say, a man who couldn't shoot geese anymore? "Stick it, Jim," I mumbled. I got off the bar stool.

"What's that?" asked Sullivan. He leaned my way.

"I said I gotta go to the john. You want to hold my hand?"

"I'll pass. I thought you said something else."

I headed for the rear of the bar. I was once able to talk to a guy like Sullivan. No more. When I got back he said his wife had called; their Pontiac still wouldn't start.

I found a pay phone and dialed home. Pamela Yew answered with her good, rich voice. "This is the Denson residence."

"Can you talk, Pamela?"

"Sure, your father's watching a football game on television. Your mother caught a ride to town with a neighbor. She didn't want to drive in the snow. She wants to buy groceries."

"Good. I may have found your Jay Hamarr. Only he doesn't call himself Hamarr anymore. He's Jerry Hammond."

"How do you know that?"

"I don't for sure; male intuition. I'll hang around another hour or two then come back. I might be able to learn something more about him."

"Thank you much, Mr. Denson."

"Later, then." I hung up.

Four

WHEN I GOT BACK to my parent's farm, Pamela Yew was peeling parsnips in the sink. My mother was stuffing a large chicken; my father was watching yet another bowl game on television. Poor Pamela. She looked surprised at the goose I had in my hand, one of Sullivan's four.

"Did you shoot that?"

I laid the goose on the counter. "No, this is one of Jim's four. I only managed to cripple one. I think I've lost the touch."

My mother began feeling the goose's breast. "Why, this one's nice. You'll have to feather and gut him."

My father looked vaguely in my direction, then returned to his game. The man on the set said Maryland had third and six on their own twenty-eight. The Terrapins broke huddle.

"Did you find your friend?" Pamela asked. She meant Jay Hamarr.

"That's probably where he was most of the morning, at Sandy's," my mother said. She didn't approve. How could I desert Pamela? Such a lovely young woman.

"No, Sandy won't be in until this evening."

Pamela understood. "You can go back by yourself later on if you'd like." She stood behind my mother and looked disgusted. Anything for dearly beloved.

"Do you mean you're going to leave Pamela here by herself?" my mother said. She liked Pamela. She didn't want me to blow it.

"That's all right, Mrs. Denson; he wants to see his friends."

I cleaned the goose and sat down by my father to watch football. He was roughly dividing his time between watching the game and Pamela Yew's rear end. After dinner I took my father's pickup to Sandy's. When I left Pamela was watching Lawrence Welk with my parents.

Sunday was a good day for Sandy Johnson. His country and western band began playing at eight o'clock. By nine thirty the place was always full. Most of the people came from across the river in Washington. They had places over there that were probably better but they liked Sandy's. The drive across the bridge made it better somehow.

Sullivan was there when I stepped into Sandy's bar. He was sitting on the same stool as though he'd never been home to start his Pontiac. He still had four geese to brag about. His story got better with the telling.

"Shit, man, did we ever have a spread. Ain't that right, Denson? They came right in on us. Never knew what hit 'em. That little pump of mine has a tight-ass choke. Reaches right up there and pops it to 'em." Sullivan was still drinking whiskey. "You have to have a tight choke for geese and you have to know how to shoot. Those bastards move faster than you think. But if you shoot too soon you can't get through the feathers. You can just hear the shot rattling off the bastards."

I nodded my head but didn't pay any attention. The tables were filling up. Soon I'd have to begin asking questions about Jerry Hammond. If he was Jay Hamarr and married to Linda Armstrong, then my trip to Cayuse was no longer a fun lark with Pamela Yew. Two single women gave me the eye while demurely drinking beer straight from the bottle. They were overweight from eating too much starch—members of the "ain't," "it don't," and "I seen" set. Their hair was lacquered into stiff, ridiculous hairdos. I had gotten up at four thirty and I needed sleep. My eyes felt like they had sand under the lids.

"Another, Sandy," said Jim Sullivan. "What about you, killer?" He was addressing me.

"Huh?"

"I mean you. Another drink?"

I didn't pay any attention. There, in the confusion of formica-topped tables and stainless-steel chairs, sat Linda Armstrong Hammond. She sipped a Tom Collins and looked my way. She was alone.

I started to get off my stool to ask her about her husband when a man appeared at the side of her table. I knew without asking that he was Jerry Hammond. I knew because of the cowboy boots. His skin-tight trousers were tucked inside the tops to show them off. Tough mothers, he would call them. He was a tough mother himself. This would be Pamela Yew's Jay Hamarr; I had no doubt of that. He had the bearing, the arrogance, the disdain of a man who placed value on no life but his own. He was at least six foot five and looked larger. His torso was a triangle from shoulders to waist. He had long arms and large hands that rested insolently on lean hips. He had two physical defects: he had small, mean eyes and the bridge of his nose was permanently swollen from having been repeatedly broken. Women would be fascinated by the broken nose. They would want to know how it got that way. They would be drawn to physical presence. They would watch his teeth. It sounds crazy, I know, but he had gorgeous teeth. The whitest teeth you ever saw.

He whispered into the ear of his wife when she suddenly flinched. She knocked over her drink.

"You don't understand," she said. She looked up at the mean little eyes.

"My lady doesn't go to bars by herself. Time you learned that, gal." The mean little eyes bore into Linda.

She stood up, only to catch Hammond's open right hand across her left ear.

Linda made a small noise. It sounded like a hiccup.

Hammond looked around him with an enormous grin. "Little bitch," he said evenly. Then he reached out in a motion I didn't know was deliberate or in anger, took the top of his

43

wife's dress with one large hand and jerked. He ripped both her dress and bra and exposed her left breast. Linda was left humiliated. She tried to cover herself but Hammond stopped her. He paused for a moment, then took his wife by the neck in what was the single most sadistic gesture I had ever seen. He slowly turned Roger Armstrong's daughter around for all to see.

The band stopped in the middle of a honky-tonk waltz; the dancers stood silent on the floor. There was one cough, nothing more.

A woman's breast. A shadow in the room.

When she came to face me, Linda's face was bunched with tears. She covered herself with her hand. I began to move in her direction but stopped when I thought I saw her shake her head no. I didn't know for sure.

"Now they all want to know what your wonderful tits look like. That's what you wanted, isn't it?" asked Jerry Hammond. He began dragging Linda to the door by her shoulder.

"I didn't know you would be home," she said. Her voice was small, intended for her husband only, but everybody in Sandy Johnson's heard it.

Sandy was suddenly there shouting at Hammond. Paunch and all, he stood right in there. In the confusion I was surprised to find Jim Sullivan shaking my shoulder.

"Well, goddamit man, get out there if you're going to," he said. Jim Sullivan would take on a Canadian goose but not Jerry Hammond. That he was leaving for me.

By the time I pushed my way through the people, Hammond had taken Linda out the front door. I stepped outside and saw Linda there, sitting on the sidewalk. Her back was against the brick facade of Sandy Johnson's and her legs were turned to one side in the snow. She was bleeding from her nose, mouth, and left ear. She dabbed at the blood on her face and stared across the street at the cemetery. The front of her dress was still open. I could see the softness of her breast under the cold white light of the fluorescent street lamp. She covered herself with her hand. She looked at me but didn't say anything.

Then I was aware of the falling snow as I had been earlier

44

in the day. It was dark. I could hear the western band inside Sandy's. It was remarkable that nobody had followed me outside. I could feel the wetness of snowflakes falling on my face.

Then a brand new Lincoln Continental pulled up at the curb. I could see Hammond's face in the darkness. Linda kept the front of her dress together with her hand.

She smiled at me with tears in her eyes, then ran to the Lincoln and opened the door on the passenger's side. I could hear the thumping beat of rock and roll music on the car radio. Hammond was tapping the steering wheel to the beat.

There was a large pair of foam-rubber dice hanging from the rearview mirror.

The next thing I knew Hammond was out of the car and coming for me. "Well, I'll be. We've got ourselves a little hero. Got the horns for sweet Linda, I'll bet."

With that he made a small motion with his right hand. I fell for it like a damned fool and caught the instep of Hammond's left boot flush on the side of my face. Damned near took my head off. I took a knee in the stomach and began a series of spastic sucking noises. My head was spinning from the booze; I couldn't breathe. I looked up to see Hammond getting ready to use my head for a soccer ball second time around. But before he got a chance a figure stepped from behind the corner of the building. Hammond half turned.

Too late.

The figure sent a wicked kick to Hammond's crotch with the arch of her foot. It was Pamela Yew, taking a shot on goal. She scored.

Hammond grabbed his testicles with both hands and pitched forward in the snow, his eyes wide with agony. He made an unintelligible gurgling sound.

Pamela helped me to my feet and half dragged, half pushed me down the slippery sidewalk to her BMW. "Stupid fool, who do you think you are, Sir Lancelot?"

I couldn't answer her. I could hardly breathe. Blood poured from my nose. I slipped out of her grasp and landed on the snow. Jerry Hammond was curled up in the fetal position in the snow holding himself; his wife stayed in his big Lincoln.

She turned to watch Pamela Yew trying to get me to her BMW.

When we got to the car, Pamela took a handful of snow and packed it over my nose. "Can you breathe?"

I nodded my head yes and breathed through my mouth.

"I don't want to get blood all over the inside of my car."

"Lovely car," I said. I was drunk on top of everything else. My head went round and round and round. I tried to focus my eyes on the knuckles of my right hand but it was no use. I couldn't fight it. I was in its grip.

Pamela was keeping an eye on Jerry Hammond, who was still on the sidewalk less than a half block away. She took her hand away from my nose. "That should stop it. Let's get out of here."

Pamela edged her BMW out into the street. I tried to stop the spinning. It wouldn't stop. The snow seemed to make it worse; the snow wanted me to look up and see it falling. I did; that made the spinning worse. The snow won. I couldn't look away.

Pamela Yew helped me up the sidewalk toward my parents' house. Before I got halfway there I slipped on the snow and fell, banging my knee painfully on the sidewalk. I sat and rubbed my knee. I felt the wet snow soaking through my trousers.

Then I puked. There in the snow, down on all fours with Pamela Yew's soft hand on the back of my neck. I vomited my guts out. I vomited and thought of Linda Hammond's breast and the foam-rubber dice in her husband's big Lincoln. I wasn't going to go back to Seattle as though nothing had happened. I couldn't do that.

The sleeping porch was unbelievably cold when we finally completed our day. The affair at Sandy Johnson's had been too much. My mouth was sour from the vomit and I was, as my old man would say, shakin' like a dog a-shittin' peach pits.

On top of that I had a broken tooth.

I was still shuddering when I climbed into bed. Pamela turned the blanket on high and slipped in. She reached out for my right hand and held it tightly for a moment.

"I want you to know I think you're a cut above those people

who stayed inside. You knew what was the right thing to do."

"Just like John Wayne."

"You go to sleep now, Mr. Denson."

I waited, riding the spinning. When it stopped I fell asleep.

When I woke it was late in the morning. I had a headache and a swollen mouth. Pamela was gone but the bed was warm; thank the man who invented the electric blanket. It had stopped snowing and had turned bitter cold. I hadn't finished dressing yet when Pamela joined me from the house.

She grinned and shook her head when she saw the side of my face. "You look lovely this morning, Mr. Denson."

I ran my fingers gingerly down the swollen side of my face. "Maybe thanks to you that I'm here at all. Where did you learn to kick like that?"

She stretched out her right leg. "Instinct."

"You just kicked."

She laughed. "Kicked where it hurts the most. Not a bad job either, I don't think. You want to tell me what motivated your John Wayne act? I can't believe you rise manfully in defense of every blonde you happen to see in a bar."

I told her my relationship with the Armstrong girls and their father. She sat on the edge of the bed and listened, staring at the dim interior of the porch that had been my bedroom as a boy. "It was a point of honor. Honor means something to me."

"We're a whole lot alike, I think."

"What I think now, Ms. Yew, is that I should slip on up to Cayuse and ask Sandy Johnson a couple of questions straight out. I know it's New Year's Eve; we'll do something thrilling tonight."

Pamela leaned forward to inspect my mashed lip close up. She poked at it gently with her finger. "Try not to be gone too long, will you? I'm getting cabin fever holed up here with your parents. I can tolerate a football game on television but your father's too much. Do you know there are Tangerine bowls, Astro-Bluebonnet bowls, Sun bowls, Peach bowls, Fiesta bowls, and Liberty bowls in addition to Blue-Gray and East-

West Shrine games? If we stay long enough there'll be sugar, cotton, roses and oranges as well."

"You forgot professional football."

Pamela took a deep breath. "Oh, yes. There are all those playoff games."

"I'll be back soon. I'll get you out of here tonight."

I took my father's pickup to Sandy's. It was slow going; the snow was packed on the highway and slippery as hell. Sandy was behind the bar as usual. He only had three customers. They worked with cattle and had crap on their jeans, western shirts, and big hats. It's an outfit you earn the right to wear. Only a real cowboy knows how to tilt his hat on the back of his head and look downright mean.

"Oh, boy, what happened to you?" Sandy grinned and leaned over the bar to examine my mouth. First Pamela, now him; I had a fun-looking lip.

"Jerry Hammond used my head for a soccer ball after I followed him out of here last night. What can you tell me about Linda Armstrong Hammond and her twin?"

Sandy looked at the cowboys, then back at me. "If I were you, I'd forget the whole thing. Last night was just a mild demonstration of Jerry Hammond's talents."

"What do you mean?" I asked.

"Buddy, you ain't the first person to get his mouth busted up by Jerry Hammond's cowboy boots."

"How about Leanne?"

"What about her?"

"Does she know her sister's situation?"

"More than you might suppose. If you really want to know, take your intended over to Bimbo's tonight. Their stripper for this week is a gal who calls herself Sweet Sally. Starts tonight. Leanne used to wait tables for me on the cafe side, same as Linda. One day after she had moved to Seattle she dropped in to say hello, had her roommate with her. The girl on Bimbo's posters who's billed as Sweet Sally is the same girl."

"Leanne Armstrong's roommate in Seattle?"

"That's it. You should be able to take it from there. Only

48

when I met her she said she was a student at the University of Washington."

"Odd that she'd wind up dancing here."

"That's what I thought. You better get your mouth fixed."

"I will," I said. I've always hated dentists and would put off having my tooth fixed until it was absolutely driving me nuts. I drove home to keep Pamela Yew company until it was time for Bimbo's strip act.

Five

"A STRIP? YOU WANT to take me to an ass parade on New Year's Eve?" Pamela Yew looked like she was trying to suppress a yawn. "I should tell you, Mr. Denson, that I've been around that kind of thing before and don't find it especially entertaining."

"I guess it all depends on how much you want to find out about Jerry Hammond, or Hamarr if that's who he is. I can always go by myself."

"I'm surprised they have that kind of thing in a drinkwater place like this."

"Good wholesome fun."

She gave me a look. "Sure it is." The University of Maryland lined up in punt formation on the television screen. "I'd almost rather watch another ball game with your father."

The punter got off what the announcer described as "another great kick."

"Well, whatever," I said.

"I'll take the stripper. It'll get me out of this house." Poor woman—some choice.

The owner of Bimbo's was an enormous Basque who was said to have once been a sheepherder in Idaho. How he came to own a bar along the river was anybody's guess. He was middle aged now and had an enlarged photograph behind the bar of himself as a young man anchoring a tug-of-war team. He was a smart bartender. He poured long, which brought back the customers. But tonight he had his problems. He had a packed house for New Year's Eve, and Sweet Sally, who was to begin her run at Bimbo's that evening, had not shown for her first turn on the floor at nine thirty. The farmers and cowboys were getting restless. The wives and girlfriends took it in stride.

At ten o'clock, the Basque announced that Sweet Sally had arrived by cab: the show would begin shortly. That brought applause and some raised eyebrows; the nearest town that boasted a taxi was thirty-five miles away. The Basque, of course, was showing them his willingness to go to any lengths to get the promised show on the road. I suspected the truth was that the Basque's girlfriend had made the run in her old Ford. She waited tables for him as well as slept with him. I hadn't seen her working that night.

Pamela Yew had come dressed to the nines, clearly in a higher league than the local talent. The hayseeds gawked. I hoped I wouldn't have to risk the unbruised side of my face in her defense.

"How was it you escaped all this, Mr. Denson?"

I laughed. "My father worked with his hands all his life. My two brothers worked with their hands. The people I went to high school with worked with their hands. I wanted out, out of that, out of the wind, out of the sand, out of the boredom. I left. I test well, Ms. Yew, the government paid for my education."

"Never looked back?"

"Never looked back. Try not to let the hayseed stares get the best of you. You have to remember that you're an exotic in a place like this."

She smiled. "I understand."

The band, whose members had separated in order to bullshit with the best-looking single women in the audience, returned to the diminutive bandstand. The lead guitarist adjusted the crotch of his pants and pulled a stubby of Blitz Weinhard beer in one yank. Then he ran a scale on his electric guitar: the signal for the lights to go down.

"It's show time once again here at Bimbo's," the guitarist announced. He was in the spotlight and loved it. His red-sequined western jacket was too small for his stomach, which was stretched from beer. The jacket had large moons of sweat stains under the armpits. The band—drummer, guitar and bass —began banging and plucking at seeming random, running scales to justify the impending entrance of that night's lovely.

"Di . . . rect from Las Ve . . . gaaas!" The guitarist thought he was really being a showman. Las Vegas to Cayuse? Everyone had to smile at that. But they didn't care. They were having a good time.

"Sah . . .weeet Sa . . . llly!"

Yes sir, it was time, friends.

The sweaty drummer began whacking and thumping like a man possessed. The bassist showed he knew his scales; his fingers were as nimble as tire irons. The lead guitarist, a trifle fuzzy from having emptied a stubby in one pull, led the way.

The show was ready to go.

Pamela Yew was fascinated by the monumental bad taste of this country schmaltz.

All heads turned now to follow the entrance of Sweet Sally, whose dressing room was located between the men's and women's toilets to cut down on plumbing costs.

"Je . . . suz Chee . . . rist!" someone said.

"My heavens!" said Pamela. She turned to meet my eyes. "Is this usual?"

Sweet Sally wasn't your average stripper. What she was doing in this joint was anybody's guess. Those who were seated in the back stood up, one-dollar beers in hand, to get a better look. That was a tip right there. Usually they stay seated, extra cool, to show they don't really give a damn about the strip. That means a lot of subtle leaning and shifting to get a better shot through the crowd.

Not this time; they were on their feet.

Nervous laughter fluttered through the darkened room.

If Sweet Sally heard a word she didn't show it. She didn't seem all that comfortable or even certain of what she was going to do next. She was stunning, there was no doubt of that. She was a natural blonde, about six feet tall, who wore high heels to accentuate her rear end and long legs. She didn't belong in a striptease act unless she was a mental case.

There's nothing especially erotic about some jaded old broad who's been there a hundred times before. This girl was different. There was something innocent about her entrance. I had a seat by the makeshift aisle that had been cleared for her entrance. She was trying terribly hard to conceal her embarrassment at having to scan faces for the cliché boobs-in-the-face bit.

Pamela caught the girl's attention with her eyes and motioned to me. "Use him, Sally. If he gets smart, I'll break his neck."

Sally looked at me.

"I'm also a friend of Leanne Armstrong," I said.

She didn't say anything but backed off and grinned at the crowd before she moved in on me, shaking her breasts this way and that.

"Those things are marvelous but you don't have to overdo it," I said.

"I have to make it look realistic." She moved closer yet and gave me a couple of tentative bumps in the face.

"Contain yourself, Mr. Denson," said Pamela Yew.

"Thank you for not being a jerk," said Sweet Sally. The rubes thought she was really giving them their money's worth. I could hear some whoops behind me from men who thought I had propositioned her. Their lady friends either stared into their drinks or watched what they thought was Sally's gall with fascination and in some cases admiration as well.

"My friend and I want to ask you some questions about Jerry Hammond."

Sweet Sally was slinging them back and forth with abandon but she listened to every word I said. "I'll be back," she said and withdrew her frontage to the cheers of the cowboys.

53

I was considered a good old boy for going along with the show. Some of the cheers were for me.

Sweet Sally was extraordinary for several reasons. One, she was young—in her mid-twenties—and a knockout. Two, she could actually dance. Both were rare for strippers. But Sally had not learned her routine on the ramps. Although few of the farmers and cowboys realized it, they were being introduced to modern dance. The cowboy music didn't make her job any easier but she was marvelous to watch.

There was a third reason why Sally was an extraordinary stripper. At least in Yawkukyl County.

Her initial embarrassment disappeared after a couple of minutes and she began to have a genuine good time—as though it was a lark. She was determined to be as scandalous and shocking as possible. She looked out into the audience, smiling, and with aplomb appropriate to the most jaded stripper in the business, plucked first one, then the other pastie from her nipples and flipped them casually into the audience. Which was agog. And which leaned forward. Pasties were required by county law.

But it was no two-second finale after which the lights were doused. No, sir. Sweet Sally kept stripping and leaping gracefully across the beer-stained dance floor.

Pamela Yew looked at me for my reaction.

"She's not a stripper; she's here for some other reason," I said.

The dancer was soon down to a gold armband, black velvet strap around her throat and a velvet G-string. The G-string had a triangular patch of inch-long tassels in front which were meant to suggest pubic hair. The tassels flopped suggestively to the movement of her slender hips.

Several people in the audience, including me, turned to see what the Basque would do after the pasties flew. He stood up on the bottom rung of his stool behind the bar. He kept working the stage lights from a portable control panel, but had a wild and helpless look in his eye. He didn't know what to do. What if there was a nut in the audience who got freaked by the idea of a bare nipple? His license was on the line. He hadn't had time to tell Sally the rules; he no doubt assumed she knew them. In any event there she was, with naked breasts and tasseled crotch.

The guitarist, I could see, was grinning broadly in the shadows of his small, raised platform. He put what seemed to be genuine enthusiasm in his play; it wasn't *his* liquor license.

The Basque apparently decided nothing could be done so he settled back on his stool, grinding his jaws and working the lights.

The band went on a break after Sweet Sally's bravura performance. A few minutes later she stood at my table dressed in a white outfit that flowed in silky shimmers from its high collar to the floor. A real clinger.

"I'd like to thank you for your help," she said.

"Oh, that was okay. I'd like you to meet my friend, Pamela Yew. My name is John Denson."

"You said you were a friend of Leanne Armstrong's?"

"Yes, I am. Would you like a drink?"

"No, thanks; the owner here just told me I wasn't to accept any drinks—among other instructions." She grinned.

"I can imagine," I said.

"Is he still sweating from your performance?" asked Pamela.

"He should probably change his shirt."

"Pamela and I have reason to believe Hammond's real name is Jay Hamarr."

Sally looked puzzled. "I thought you were trying to find Leanne."

Pamela touched my shoulder, a signal for me to shut my ignorant mouth. "Is Leanne missing?"

Sally paused, apparently uncertain of what she should say next. "Well, Mr. Denson, your friend Leanne used to be my roommate at the University of Washington. She plays around with dope and, how do I say it, shares that man Hammond with her sister. Yes, she's missing. She's in a pack of trouble. More than you or I or anybody else can do a thing about."

"We may be able to do something about it," said Pamela.

"How's that?"

"Mr. Denson and I are both private investigators."

"You're a detective?" She looked at Pamela.

Pamela laughed. "Yes, but I'll bet you're not a stripper by profession, are you?"

"Heavens, no. I was scared to death when I came out here tonight but it wasn't so bad once I got going."

"Will you talk to us about your friend Leanne and Jerry Hammond?"

Sally looked around Bimbo's. "After I get off work tonight. I have one more show at eleven."

"Thank you," said Pamela.

Sally smiled and leaned closer. "Did you two like my dancing?"

"You wowed 'em," I said.

"Terrific, if you go for that sort of thing," said Pamela.

"No kidding, did you really like it? I know it's awful but I've got a bet going."

I shrugged my shoulders. "I said it was good and I meant it."

Sally looked suspicious. "Have you seen many strippers before?"

"Sure. I've seen them in Baltimore, L. A., lots of places." I hated to admit that in front of Pamela. "But that was when I was younger." Pamela had an uh, huh expression on her face.

"How did I stack up?"

"I've never seen better."

"Really? And was I sexy, do you think?"

"You wouldn't have to strip to do that."

"I think I almost blew that Basque's mind." She laughed. "He was worrying about getting his money's worth."

She almost blew the Basque's customers' minds at eleven p.m. But with pasties. It was a few minutes after her last performance that all the lights in Bimbo's went on unexpectedly. The Basque's customers looked around in confusion—it wasn't closing time yet.

The Basque himself ran toward Sweet Sally's dressing room. Just then Pamela was nearly flattened by a jerk wearing a snappy green fedora. He crashed into me as well. He gave us both the eyeball on the way past.

"Oh, my God," he muttered. In seconds he was on the heels of the Basque, who looked stricken.

I caught Pamela's eye.

"He thinks we're a handsome couple, maybe," she said.

A few minutes later everybody was talking about what had happened. Sweet Sally, the stripper who was not a stripper, had been found slumped over her dressing table with her throat cut. Nobody had seen her murderer.

Then the local fuzz showed up, an overweight cop with a W. C. Fields nose. He had sense enough to get the names and addresses of everybody present. It took Pamela and me an hour and a half to get out of Bimbo's. We were lucky; we were among the first interviewed. The man in the fedora watched us all the while.

"Maybe he's interested in sort of *ménage à trois,*" said Pamela.

"It'd have to be two ladies and me; you can tell him that if you like."

"I'll pass."

As we left, Pamela tapped me on the shoulder. "Look there, our friend, Mr. Hamarr."

Jerry Hammond was standing across the street from the tavern. I don't think he saw us—or paid attention to anybody for that matter.

Hammond urinated on the sidewalk and grinned at the cars going by slowly on the icy streets. It was his idea of beginning the New Year right.

Six

PAMELA AND I WERE bedded down, divided by our platonic 38th Parallel, when I felt there was someone with us on the sleeping porch. I didn't know whether it was a dream or not. It was one of those cases where you don't know for sure and it scares you. Then I knew I was awake. I had to go to the john. I was sure it was a dream. But then I saw a silhouette.

I found Pamela's hand and gave it a slight squeeze. She squeezed back. She was awake also.

"Take it easy, Denson." It was a man.

I didn't recognize the voice but he didn't sound like he meant to do me any harm. He moved to my left at the foot of the bed and squatted on his haunches. My mother's dog barked. A beagle with a torn ear. Why hadn't the mutt barked earlier?

"This place is cold. How do you keep warm?" he asked.

"Well, I have my lady here with me and I have an electric blanket. Who are you and what do you want?"

"Jerry Hammond," said the voice.

I felt Pamela Yew's body tense in the bed. Both of us were trapped there under blankets. "Can't this wait until tomorrow?"

He talked as if Pamela wasn't there. "You can just listen all you want, sweetheart, this here's between me and old John here."

"You broke my goddam tooth," I said by way of openers. I was pleasant enough about it under the circumstances. But I was visiting my home town from the big city and there are obligations, especially since I was a detective. The problem was I was afraid Hammond might turn sadistic, with me trapped under the blankets with Pamela Yew. If I'm careless about myself, she mattered.

"I broke your tooth; some son of a bitch broke my balls. I want to know who he was."

My heart felt like it was trying to pump molasses. Who *he* was? "I never saw him before in my life."

There was a snapping sound and a match flared. Hammond lit a cigarette. "I only saw him out of the corner of my eye. He was a skinny bastard, not very big."

"I don't know; I wasn't seeing much of anything myself."

"Wife says he had a mustache. Doesn't matter. He'll brag about it one of these days and word'll get back to me. He'll wish it hadn't. She says you're a detective." His voice had a trace of southern accent.

"Mostly I just follow women around for jealous husbands and the other way around."

"How did you get into that line of work, anyway?" The question seemed amiable enough.

"In the intelligence business," I said. "The Army sent me to a school; so did the CIA."

"I cut throats," he said. "Damned good at it too. That and shooting a pistol. Every once in a while I pranged a nigger with a pistol just for the hell of it. Damned good with a pistol."

Sweet Jesus, I thought to myself. Pamela stirred beside me.

"Where did you do that?"

"Angola. Hired out of Marseilles with a bunch of other assholes. Should've stuck to flying dope."

"How's that?" I was interested in spite of myself.

"Ain't no fun spending time in a nigger stockade. Took me six weeks to bust out."

"Oh boy," I said. "Where did you fly dope?" He was a talker, a bragger, as Sullivan had said.

59

"Golden Triangle, know what I mean—Thailand, Burma. I liked them women. Hard little bodies."

Pamela stiffened. It struck me that Hammond didn't sound bitter about being captured in Angola. He was proud of it. It was his badge of manhood—something he told everybody. Pamela Yew was in for a real treat. If I was going to be a real man in his eyes, I would have to come up with a story of my own. He waited, wondering if I had a pair. Pamela waited, curious as to how I would answer.

"I didn't get into any battles or anything. Nearest I came was laying a 175-pound WAC in a Dempster Dumpster." Pamela jabbed me in the ribs with her elbow. "Damned thing was half full of tin cans and watermelon rinds. Thirty-three of us got the clap from her. They were going to make grunts out of us until some colonel made the list. Holabird's a small place."

"Shit, man, that's a good one. Humpin' in a fuckin' metal box. That takes real hair." Hammond laughed loudly.

I was hopeful. Pamela Yew was in no position for another dramatic rescue.

"Say, how is it you know my wife?" he asked.

My blood thinned at that one. My ears thundered like timpani in a Cecil B. DeMille movie. I had to be careful. "I don't know her, really. She and her sister used to live a couple of houses down the road. I hunted geese with their old man. We were out with the sun every morning and every weekend. The twins were just little girls when I went off to college. I never came back."

"She said she saw you in Sandy Johnson's cafe yesterday morning and went back last night to look for you. Knew you'd be looking for your old pals." He shifted haunches in the darkness.

I cleared my throat. "What did she want to see me for?"

"She wanted to see you about her sister, Leanne. Leanne got a scholarship a few years back to go to the University of Washington. She wrote Linda regular. They were real close, you know. Leanne graduated in June. Linda says she ain't written in months. She's worried sick."

Pamela shifted slightly in the bed, moving toward me into the platonic no person's land. "I don't understand," I said.

"Leanne started hanging around with a crowd of longhaired punks. Dumb shits with hair down to their assholes. Linda don't know what to do."

"Maybe the two of them just grew apart. Maybe they don't have anything to write about anymore. That happens."

"Linda thought that at first but now she's certain something is wrong. You know how sisters are and all. That's why she tried to find you at Sandy Johnson's. She should've told me, saved herself a few bruises and a cracked rib."

"What does she want with me?"

"She wants you to find Leanne."

"Find Leanne?"

"That's it."

"And for that she earned a cracked rib?" Pamela Yew gave my rib a gouge for being so dumb. She was right: if I thought there was a chance that Hammond had the makings of an okay guy underneath it all, I was mistaken.

"Now you listen up, buddy, and listen real good. What happens between me and my wife ain't none of nobody's fuckin' business. Maybe next time she'll stay at home where she belongs. Rib served her right."

Pamela Yew dug her fingernails into my arm; she probably wanted them in Hammond's eyeballs. "I'll have to talk to Linda to get something to go on." I didn't know what else I could say.

"You watch ball games?"

"Sure."

"Then why don't you come on over tomorrow afternoon and watch a little football on television?" Hammond was now the gracious host. "We can drink a few beers, talk it over."

"Listen, I'm going to have to have a cap put on my tooth and . . ."

"Doc Agee lives behind his office. He's a bachelor. Won't be doing much tomorrow except drinking himself blind. He'll fix you up. Tell him to put it on my bill."

I didn't imagine he had credit with a dentist but I could feel the cold air on the broken tooth. "That sounds good."

61

"We'll see you tomorrow, hear." Hammond rose from his squat and left the porch without saying another word.

Pamela Yew returned to her side of the bed. "Now you know what the feminist movement is all about."

"We're not all that bad."

"Don't congratulate yourself yet, Mr. Denson."

After breakfast, Pamela Yew drove me to town in her BMW and I looked up Agee the dentist. His office was closed for the holidays; he was upstairs in his apartment drinking Old Crow and watching football on the tube.

"Really wasn't planning on opening up today," he said when he opened the door.

I opened my mouth so he could see my tooth. "Hurts like a bitch in this cold weather. This is my friend Pamela Yew."

He looked from tooth to Pamela. "It'll only take a few minutes, I suppose."

We went downstairs to his office. He took his bottle of Old Crow with him. He poured each of us about three fingers and offered some to Pamela but she said no with a smile.

"Ain't no day to be sober," he said. "No day at all."

I took a slug of the warm, straight whiskey and grimaced like they do in the movies. "Good stuff," I lied.

"Happy New Year!" he said. He touched his glass to mine in a holiday toast. "Here's hoping your mouth isn't too mashed up. You're lucky you can still talk."

"I want you to bill this to a fellow named Jerry Hammond. He said he'd pay."

The doc peered into my mouth. "I know. Left to him, though, I'd never get my money. He do this with his fist or did it take one of his fancy cowboy boots?"

"Cowboy boot." My mouth was contorted out of shape from his fingers. Pamela Yew took a chair by a window and looked outside at Cayuse's main street.

"That kid's handy with his feet. He should have been a soccer player or a tap dancer. You're not old Leon Denson's boy are you?"

"Ooooh! Ouch! Yes."

"I was talking to him just the other day. Says you're a

detective or something like that up in Seattle. Better take another slug of whiskey if you don't want to be shot up with a bunch of dope. The tooth's not so bad but if I shoot you with a needle, alcohol will make you sicker than a dog for the rest of the day. Hell of a holiday that would make."

I pushed backward into the chair as if I could back away from the pain. Agee was a fast worker, I'll give him that. He bore right in there without wasting time, occasionally using a jet of water to clear the mess in my mouth. Probably wanted to get back to the ball game.

"Understand you're going to help Linda Hammond find her twin sister."

"Gnnnaahhhh!" He forced my jaw back so I couldn't talk.

That didn't stop Pamela Yew from talking. "You probably know a lot about a small town like this, working on people's teeth all day."

Agee looked pleased. "Everybody knows everybody else in a place like this, Miss Yew. Not a whole lot of privacy." He laughed.

"Do you know what Jerry Hammond does in Seattle, who his friends are there?"

It was a good thing Agee had my head pinned against the headrest: there was no way Pamela could judge my reaction to her question. Why would she care what Hammond did in Cayuse or anywhere if her only purpose was to bring him to justice?

Agee removed his hands from my mouth for a moment to consider her question. "Come to think of it, I saw Linda at the grocery store a couple weeks back. She said something about Jerry's having seen the Sonics play the Knicks at the Kingdome."

"Oh," said Pamela.

"I see her around town every once in a while. Spit in the tray, John. Thank you. Linda called to say you'd be coming in to have your tooth fixed. She said she'd see to it I get my money. Didn't say how the tooth got busted but I figured that out. Nice little gals, the Armstrongs, both of them. I hate to see them all messed up."

63

"I thought you were going to drill a hole clear through my jaw."

"I've just about got it. How was it you got your face in the way of his boot?"

"His foot was moving rapidly from right to left and my face was in the way."

"People's faces have a way of getting in front of Jerry Hammond's cowboy boots. That ought to do it."

"Finished?"

"Mrs. Hammond's a mighty nice litle woman to push around like that. Hammond leaves her at home weeks at a time."

"He's a real charmer."

"He's gonna break somebody's jaw sometime. Then he'll be in real trouble. His folks moved up here from California when he was a kid. He stayed in California."

Pamela Yew stood up. "California?"

Agee nodded. "A regular CIO."

"CIO?" Pamela asked.

"California Improved Okie. Don't belong to the country. Don't belong to the city. Can't get along in either. Turns 'em mean."

I didn't say anything.

Agee poured himself another three fingers and consumed half of that in one swallow. He eyed me over the rim of the glass.

"I've been a whiskey-drinking man for some time now."

I said nothing. He wasn't a brain surgeon, after all.

"More, though, since my wife was killed. It's tough living alone, nothing to do. Damned television. She was killed three years ago in Anaheim."

"Anaheim?"

"Anaheim. That's where Disneyland is, you know. How many people you know died in Anaheim?"

"This is my first, I guess."

"She stepped off a curb and was run over by a truck full of plastic animals headed for Disneyland—the kind that move around and wave at kids. The most amazing thing you've ever seen."

"I'm sorry," I said and felt stupid saying it.

"I saw a western once where Kirk Douglas was run over by a truck loaded with toilets. The police were after him with radios, helicopters, and high-powered rifles, but they couldn't catch him. He almost had it made, when he tried to cross a highway on a rainy night. His horse was frightened by the cars and Kirk couldn't control him. Then the truck came."

"I think I saw that movie. The last cowboy and all that."

"My wife wasn't running from anything. She wasn't the last cowboy. She was just the last wife of Henry Agee. She was crossing the street to buy some chicken-flavored cat food from a Safeway. I watched the whole thing from the front seat of an Oldsmobile. Plastic animals, for God's sake. Elephants, hippos. Kirk Douglas got the better deal."

"I think he did too."

Agee took another slug of whiskey. He twirled the ice in the bottom of his glass.

"How did you happen to move up here?"

"I sued the trucking company but didn't get anywhere. Then I had a bachelor cousin die here and he left me a farm. That was the same day I saw an ad in the papers telling about a new Disney movie; I think it was called 'Bambi and the Leprechauns in Outer Space.' The animals in the newspaper ad looked like those animals on the back of the truck. That did it. I figured, What the hell, people have teeth up here too and the whiskey tastes just as good. Been here six years now."

"What happened to the farm?"

Agee began putting his tools away. "You ever farmed?"

"No, drove truck in the peas and wheat."

"You have any idea what a person's supposed to do with a hundred acres of watermelons?"

"Watermelons?"

"That's right, a hundred acres."

"No, I guess I don't."

"Neither did I."

"So you sold it?"

"Sold it. Have some more whiskey."

"I think I've had enough."

We said our goodbyes to Agee and Pamela Yew trailed after me to the Fiat. My mouth was swollen and my bruised lips throbbed.

"Well, now's your chance to meet Jerry Hammond," I said.

"I think I'll pass on the opportunity, Mr. Denson. I'm not feeling well."

"They only live a half mile from here and it shouldn't take long, fifteeen or twenty minutes."

Pamela Yew wrapped her woolen scarf more tightly around her throat. "I'd just as soon not, Mr. Denson."

"It's three miles out and three miles back to my parents home."

"I'm not feeling well."

"There's no reason not to meet him if all you're going to do is turn him over to the cops."

The ball was squarely in her court. "I said I don't feel well, Mr. Denson. Will you please take me home?" Her voice rose, pausing at the edge of anger.

I drove her back to my parent's house, wondering about the real reason for Pamela Yew's visit to Cayuse, Oregon.

Linda Hammond and her husband lived by the river in a small yellow house with peeling paint. Hammond's big Lincoln with the foam-rubber dice was parked out front. Linda answered my knock. She wore a light dress that showed the profile of a safety pin holding her bra together in the back.

"Won't you come in, John. I see it's starting to snow again."

She had a smile that was open and direct. She lacked guile and maybe because of that had become a doormat for a jerk. There is no describing my rage at Hammond. I stepped inside. I could hear the Trojans of the University of Southern California being introduced on the television set.

"That's some shiner you've got. Walk into a door?" I smiled.

She felt her eye with the back of her hand. "How about your mouth?" she laughed.

"Come on in and take a load off," Hammond yelled without getting out of his easy chair. "Get him a beer, Linda."

She brought me a 16-ounce can of Blitz Weinhard; I sat

66

down in a chair with a rip in the arm. Hammond ignored us. I could smell pie cooking in the next room.

"I can't stay too long," I said.

"We're going over to Jerry's parents after the game," Linda said.

"He doesn't want to hear that crap. Tell him about Leanne." Hammond didn't look at us. The Trojans won the toss.

"Do you think you can find her, John?"

"I don't know. That depends, I guess. Seattle's a large city. I've been getting a lot of work looking for runaways lately and I know some places to check. Do you have a picture of her?"

"She looks just like me." Linda smiled.

"I'll need the picture to show others. They don't know what you look like."

"Oh, I see." She got up to get a picture. "I don't have a recent one of Leanne but maybe this one of me will do."

"Now is there anything at all which might help me out, the name of a boyfriend or girlfriend, anything?"

"No. We wrote to each other once a week until July, when the letters stopped coming. She asked me for money a couple of times before she stopped writing. She'd never done that before."

"How much did she ask for?"

"Well, the last time she asked for five hundred dollars. She didn't say what she wanted it for. There was no way I could get that kind of money by waitressing." She looked at Jerry to see if he had heard but he wasn't paying any attention; the Trojans crossed midfield.

"Do you know if she had a job?"

"No. She graduated in June from the University of Washington; she had several offers of aid to go to graduate school. I think for a while she was thinking about studying for a Ph.D. in art history at UCLA. Then she got caught up in mysticism and the rest of it."

"The rest of what?"

"You know."

"I'm not sure I do. You'll have to be as specific as possible."

"She was running around with an artist named Larry Fowler

67

and his friends. I think she earned a few dollars posing in the nude." Linda blushed slightly at that.

"Did she say where she modeled?" Odd coincidence, Pamela Yew and the artist business.

Linda looked at the floor. "I think it was someplace near the university."

"Did she mess around with dope?"

"I don't know."

If she didn't know for sure, Linda suspected it. That much was clear from her face.

"I'll also need part of a letter from her to you—for the handwriting. And I'll need her last known address."

Linda got me a letter. "How much will all this cost?" she asked. She was nervous. She didn't want to ask the question.

For the first time, Jerry Hammond looked up from the television set. It was a remarkable effort. The Trojans were third and goal to go on the Buckeye seven. Curt Gowdy was describing the action.

"The Trojans would like to come away with a touchdown on this drive," Gowdy said.

Hammond watched me, waiting for an answer to Linda's question.

"That's okay, I can work it into the rest of my comings and goings," I said.

Hammond flashed his beautiful teeth with a great big grin. The Trojan quarterback had called time out; Hammond had a minute to spare. Curt Gowdy's partner explained to the fans why seven points were better than three, then it was on to a beer commercial.

"Say, you play ball in high school, Denson?"

"I was a wingback," I said. "I was small but slow."

"They say Mungo still ran the single-wing in your days?"

"I learned to like blocking."

"I was a tailback. Made Shriners in California. You don't look all that big."

"Mungo said I had a lot of heart, whatever that means."

"I remember you playing," said Linda. "My cousin was in

68

your class, Billy Barnes. We went to all the games to see Billy play."

"He was a tackle on the left side."

"I'll bet he was a mean son of a bitch," said Hammond. He shook his head and had a vacant look in his eye which meant, I knew, that he was remembering once again those touchdowns and golden days of yore. Newspaper clippings and Shriners to top it off. He lived in the past and punished the present. A high school football hero who would never forget and never grow up.

"I also remember you on the basketball team. You spent all your time on the bench." Linda smiled.

"More heart again," I said.

"Denson?" It was Hammond.

"Yeah?"

"The minute you find Leanne, and I mean the very minute, I want you to give me a call, hear? Immediately."

"Sure," I said. I didn't know what else to say. He flashed those damned white teeth at me. I sat there looking dumb.

"Don't fuck around now. I want you on that horn fast." He turned back to the television set.

The Trojans broke huddle.

I drove back to my parents' house. Pamela Yew was in the bathroom combing her hair. The door was open so I leaned in. "Truth time, Pamela Yew. I think we need to go for a little drive."

She put her brush away without saying anything and followed me to the BMW. It was snowing again; there must have been a foot-and-a-half accumulation. Neither Pamela nor I said anything as I eased the car down the slippery main street of Cayuse, watching for a phone booth. I found one by a Texaco station.

"I have to make a phone call, I'll only be a minute," I said. I pulled to the side of the road.

"Phone call, Mr. Denson?"

"I'm wondering about artists, missing women, Seattle, and a detective named Yew. I'm wondering why you didn't want Jerry Hammond to get a look at you."

"I see."

I waded through the snow, slipped into the glass booth, gave the operator my credit card number, and phoned Capt. James Gilberto of the Seattle Police Department.

"Administration, Captain Gilberto here."

"Hey, Jim. Gumshoe John."

"Dammit, I thought maybe you'd been drowned in Lake Washington or something. What is it you want, Gumshoe?" Gilberto laughed his wheezing giggle of a laugh.

"Just want to pick your memory, Jim. I want to know about a case in San Francisco where a pimp beat up and maimed a call girl, then murdered the witnesses one by one over a period of two or three years?"

"Sure, I know that one. What do you want to know?"

"I want to know what happened in the case. Do they have a suspect or any solid evidence?"

"Oh, yeah, they got solid evidence okay. They caught the guy and convicted him. He's in San Quentin if you want to talk to him."

Pamela Yew was watching me from her BMW. "What was his name, can you remember?"

"Sure, I remember, the detective who solved the case talked about it at a police workshop in Los Angeles last summer. The killer was a black pimp named Robert Carroll, Bobby Carroll."

"Does the name Jerry Hammond mean anything to you?"

Gilberto thought that over a minute. "I've heard it but I can't tell you where."

"That's square, thanks, Jim." I hung up and waded back through the snow to the BMW. I got in, took a deep breath, closed my eyes and let the air out slowly. "Bobby Carroll."

Pamela Yew's left eyebrow raised.

"A black man named Bobby Carroll killed those girls, Pamela."

"You are a detective, after all, Mr. Denson." She laughed.

"I've been had."

"If you mean you fell for a good line, yes, you were."

"So what is it you're after?"

70

Pamela Yew looked surprised. "You gotta be kidding. You have to find that out for yourself; I'm not going to tell you."

"I'll tell you something, Ms. Yew. This isn't my idea of any way to do business. You want to play a man's game you don't pull stunts like that."

"Right out front, eh, Mr. Denson?"

"Right out front."

"Sure," she said. "You guys are all the time straight arrow. Man's game. Tell me about it."

"I'm not 'you guys.' I'm me."

Pamela Yew looked at me evenly. "I hired you to squire me into this pathetic town, Mr. Denson, and you'll get your money. I'm paying you well. What I'm after is my business, my business alone."

"It has to be worth money or you would have squared with me from the beginning." I glared at her.

Pamela Yew didn't say anything.

"That's not how I deal with people," I said.

She shrugged her shoulders. "Would you have told me?"

"You're damned right I would have."

"I don't think so, Mr. Denson. I think you'd have done exactly as I did."

"Then you don't even begin to know me."

She shrugged again.

"As far as I'm concerned you can take your payoff and stick it."

She smiled. "Oo, no. I don't think so. I was thinking more in terms of an Alfa Spider, maybe, and a few months on the Mediterranean, something like that."

I should have let it sit right there. I knew that, knew I should have kept my mouth shut. Knew it from having faced down an intelligence officer named Adrian Kile in London. Knew it from having mouthed off to a newspaper editor named Tom Becker in Honolulu. Thus endeth two careers: one for having refused to murder a man; the other for refusing to back off a hunch about the *Glomar Challenger*. I was right about *Glomar;* the government wasn't trying to bore into the center of the earth at all; it was trying to raise a sunken Soviet sub-

71

marine. My parting shot at Becker was cute: "Tom, I don't give a damn about going to cocktail parties with admirals or having dinner with the governor. I just care about being a good newspaperman and doing a job for my readers."

Thus it was that I tried to wing it as a freelance, which didn't work out because I liked to eat occasionally. I wound up chasing arsonists for insurance companies and wayward wives for irate husbands.

I wasn't willing to back down. It was a fault; I'd be competitive to my grave. I looked outside at the snow and took a deep breath. "I'd like to make you a little bet, Ms. Yew," I said without turning to face her.

"A bet?" she asked behind my back. "Why what kind of bet, Mr. Denson?"

"Tell you what, Ms. Detective. I'll bet you that I'll beat you to whatever it is you're after and collect the payoff."

Pamela Yew didn't laugh. "You're betting you're a better man than I am."

"Exactly."

I felt a finger tap me on the spine. "Take a look, Mr. Denson." I looked. "I'm a woman, Mr. Denson."

"You know what I meant. I meant I'm betting I'm a better detective than you are. I don't like your little fraud."

"I know what you said, I can only guess at what you meant." She looked down at her breasts. "These things haven't gotten in my way yet. Just what is it you want to bet, Mr. Denson?"

I shrugged. "You bring sex into it, sex you'll get. If I win, Ms. Yew, I get a non-platonic weekend with you. Dinner on a Friday night would be nice for starters. I'm partial to Japanese restaurants. Then we'd snuggle a little and whisper sweet nothings to one another." I stopped here and looked thoughtful. "Breakfast in bed would be fun, *huevos rancheros* for me and good coffee with cream."

"Followed by an afternoon delight," Pamela offered.

"Oh yes." I grinned. "That would be nice indeed! We shouldn't hurry anything, mind you. Take our time."

"Uh huh."

"That night there'd be fried razor clams at Ivar's followed

by a Sonics ball game, watch Freddie Brown pump 'em in from downtown."

"I'd fetch the beer."

"And the peanuts, I like peanuts. Peanuts make me horny."

Pamela Yew's eyes narrowed perceptively. "The bottom line, Mr. Denson, is that you want to bed me down."

"Precisely." I was so enraged I could hardly see.

"What you think I need is a good screw, eh, for having the gall to compete with you and Sam Spade."

"I didn't say that."

"I did." Pamela was as hot as I was. "What if I win? What do I get?"

I turned both palms up. Mr. Generosity. "You name it, love."

"If I win, John Denson, I want your original Thomas Eakins."

"The hell you say." I couldn't believe she'd said that. "Listen lady, that painting's worth fifty thousand bucks and you know it. Maybe more."

She shrugged her shoulders and looked indifferent. "Well, you're the one who's the big gambler. You'll have to decide what I'm worth." She looked down at herself again. "Nothing here no other woman has. I think you'd be nuts to accept but if you're so good and all."

"Damned good," I said.

"Well, you know what you want, I know what I want."

"No deal."

"I thought as much." Her smile was infuriating.

"Do you really think a turn in bed with you is worth fifty thousand bucks?"

She grinned. "No. I didn't say that. I simply said that's my price. Everybody has a price. For you, Mr. Denson, that's mine. I want to see if you have—yes, I want to see if you have the balls."

"No deal."

"Oh, come on now, Mr. Denson. Humphrey Bogart beat Sydney Greenstreet and Peter Lorre to the Maltese Falcon. After all . . ." Her voice trailed off. She'd made her challenge.

She knew how to make me twist. Pamela Yew wanted my Eakins.

"Done." It was automatic. I immediately regretted it.

She extended her hand.

I took it.

Pamela Yew beamed. She whacked herself on the side of her hip. "Fifty thousand bucks, not bad for a thirty-six-year-old, eh?"

I stared at the floorboards of her BMW. "Well, you've got your hustle. Will you give me any help? After all, you have a tremendous head start? If you had a pair you'd make it even up."

She laughed. "Ah, but I don't, Mr. Denson. Not of those anyway. A bet's a bet. Don't be a whiner."

I ran my fingers across my chin. "Anatomy is not the point, Ms. Yew. Fair play is. Person, place or thing? Animal, mineral or vegetable?"

She laughed. "Okay then, never let it be said that I took refuge behind sex. Thing mineral."

"Thing mineral it is. I want to see some enthusiasm on our date."

"Mr. Denson, in that unlikely event I promise to do my very best."

"I can't wait." I grinned.

Pamela Yew shook her head. "We'll see, Mr. Denson." She started her BMW and we returned to my parents' house to pack for the trip back to Seattle.

I knew thing mineral would be found in Seattle.

Seven

WE LEFT AN HOUR LATER. The radio said Snoqualmie Pass was still fouled with snow, so Pamela turned the BMW down the gorge again; Portland would be the first stop, halfway there. That wasn't much better. There was only one lane open on each side of the Interstate.

"So it was the name of the girl you were after, eh, Ms. Yew."

She grinned. "I've told you all I'm going to tell you. We can chat amiably about the weather. We can sit in silence. Or we can listen to that awful country music on the radio."

"All I have to do is find the girl."

Pamela Yew did her eyebrow number. "You don't even know what you're looking for. Nobody's going to volunteer the information, I can assure you."

"It's a miserable day out."

"Awful."

We drove in silence.

"That about takes care of the weather," I said.

"I think so."

We listened to country music until the stations faded in the gorge. After that we played poker with automobile license plates. It was late at night when we got into Seattle. Pamela Yew took me to my office where my Fiat was parked.

"I suppose I'll be seeing you here and there," I said, when I had my bags on the sidewalk.

"I suppose." She grinned.

I leaned through the open window and surprised her with a little kiss.

"Don't be premature now, Mr. Denson." She smiled and drove off.

I drove my Fiat back to my apartment for some sleep before the competition began.

Before I used my key I tried Winston, my doorbell—doordog actually. Winston was a stuffed English pit bull I bought at an auction in Baltimore. He was a terrible-looking thing, sitting tensed on his haunches ready to spring, glaring up at his adversary with bared fangs and hateful eyes. I put Winston in a lean-to doghouse by my front door and wired him to a tape machine and a button on my door. Visitors were confronted with the malevolent Winston who growled a vicious, vengeful growl when they tried the button on the door. I liked it a lot.

Even better was when my visitors opened the door. Winston stopped abruptly when the door opened, giving way to taped jungle sounds in my apartment—parrots and macaws screaming, monkeys chattering, the works. Following Winston's performance, it was marvelous.

Then there was the apartment itself, the walls of which were cluttered with souvenirs, photographs of heroes and villains, and memorabilia from my past. It was my ambition to one day cause the walls to disappear altogether.

The walls contained the usual as well as the unexpected. There was my bachelor's degree from Reed College, of course, and my master's degree in journalism from American University, a picture of me at age three sitting naked on a flat rock with a lizard in my hand. That kind of thing and more. There was a glassed frame of arrowheads I had found on the banks of the Columbia River when I was a kid. There was a map—illustrated with colored pullovers—of the English 1st Division. There was a photograph of myself and Steve Graham, a top officer in the CIA, drinking calvados at a Paris sidewalk cafe. I had on the wall a print of a painting, author unknown, portraying the death of Lord Nelson. There were newspaper photographs of Ernest Hemingway fishing for tarpon off the Florida Keys and Harry Truman holding a copy of the *Chicago Tribune* declaring Thomas Dewey the winner of the presidential election of 1948. I had mounted black and white glossies of Nellie Fox at bat for the Chicago White Sox in the 1959 World Series, Paul Hornung scoring a touchdown for the Green Bay Packers, and Gordon Banks making a save against a Dutch striker. I had a picture of myself in the city room of the morning daily in Honolulu with a lady in a bikini on my lap, a picture of me and a Chinese girl with whom I once lived for three months in Hong Kong, and a picture of me at age fifteen, holding a fifteen-pound steelhead, my thumb through its gills.

I had an English dart board, a dozen dart trophies, a picture of me eating a giant hot dog heaped with chopped raw onions. There were pictures, also, of a man in a bowling shirt that featured a naked lady on a zebra, and Eugene McCarthy posing with a first baseman's mitt. Then there were the posters: the Kingston Trio; Slim Pickens portraying Major Kong in the movie "Dr. Strangelove"; and a fabulous female butt. Above, model airplanes hanging from the ceiling attacked the walls from various angles: American P-38's, Japanese Zeros, German Messerschmits. I had Richard Nixon crawling out of a manhole in a Herblock cartoon amidst boomerangs, a two-shot derringer in a wrist holster, a Norwegian flag, a metal school bus, and a rear tire tacked to the wall.

That's not to mention my prizes: Denson watercolor #16, painted at the beach at Westport, Washington, and the loons I had carved and painted.

One thing I like to do before settling down to a case is make sure I've taken care of naggling little details like the laundry. I checked my supply of corduroy pants: fine. Corduroy jackets: fine. Cotton shirts: okay. Sweaters: clean. Then there was the question of which Irish walking hat I would wear for this case: gray or brown. I decided on the brown but needed a new look for luck. I steamed it over the teakettle, poked it into a rumpled shape, and put it in the freezing compartment of my refrigerator. It would be ready in the morning.

That done I opened a bottle of Mackeson's stout and studied the walls, wondering what new additions I would make as a result of my meeting Pamela Yew.

The next morning I called Emma at my answering service. In addition to taking calls for me, Emma kept in touch with Sheila, my niece, who earned pocket money doing research for me. Sheila was a student at the University of Washington. In the last couple of years Sheila and Emma had become friends over the telephone; Sheila was convinced Emma was in love with me—or maybe her idea of what I was like. I'd seen Emma just once. She was slender and a bit shy. She had a marvelous telephone voice. I suspected she was bored, lonely, and maybe a bit trapped by life. I also suspected she was a reader of Kahlil Gibran. I had thought more than once about asking her out for a drink or something but I just don't have the stuff for a Gibran lover.

"Hello, Emma, love. Happy New Year!"

"Why, hello, Mr. Denson." Emma giggled. "A Happy New Year to you, too. Did you have a nice holiday in Cayuse?"

"Oh, sure, sure, Emma; it was fun. Is Sheila back at school?"

"She's back, Mr. Denson. Her classes start tomorrow. She checked in yesterday afternoon. I told her you had nothing for her as far as I knew."

"Tell her to keep in touch. Something's going on here, and I might need some information later."

"Everything's okay with you, isn't it, Mr. Denson?"

"I'm fine, Emma. I won't be coming into my office for a few more days. Save my calls. I'll keep in touch."

"You're not in trouble or anything?" Emma had an acute desire to have things spelled out for her. Gibran will do that to you.

"Thank you for your concern, Emma." I hung up. There was much about the Leanne Armstrong business—the murderous Hammond, the dead stripper, my suspicions about Pamela Yew —that should have made me drop everything right there. But I had a bet. I'd do my damndest to win it.

My first step was to take a little drive. Pamela Yew followed me, not doing badly. She wasn't as good as I was but she held

78

her own. I decided to let her stay and drove out to check the address Linda had given me. It turned out to be an old white house in the university district, possibly built in the 1930s.

The house was curtainless and empty. The front door was locked but I found a side window that was opened a crack to let the air circulate. I took a quick look around, opened the window and hoisted myself through. My footsteps echoed on the worn hardwood floor as I nosed about looking for something to go on. Nothing there but a telephone directory. Most people have bad memories for telephone numbers and cheat in all kinds of ways. I took the directory and left a message in its place: "Didn't find anything. Took the phone directory with me. Maybe there'll be something there. John."

I slipped out through a back door, returned to my Fiat and drove to a Szechwan Chinese restaurant for some twice-fried pork. I didn't check to see if Pamela Yew was behind me when I left. She was apparently determined to let me do her work for her. I didn't care. I bought myself a couple of bottles of San Miguel dark and went to my apartment to see if I could find any leads in the telephone book. It was getting on in the evening, a good time for the telephone: hit 'em at prime television time.

There were six names penciled in the front page. I called each one, asked for Leanne Armstrong, got no for an answer, and recorded them in my notebook. Then I began with page one and checked each page for checks or marks. On page 137 I found an underlined number. I gave it a try:

"May I speak to Leanne, please."

"Leanne . . ." The other party, a man, paused and hung up. He knew the name Leanne.

Voila! I was ahead of Pamela Yew.

I got in my Fiat and headed across town. Pamela was behind me in her BMW but I gave her the slip. It was almost midnight when I pulled in behind a yellow Porsche parked in front of the apartment building.

I pushed the buzzer and waited.

The door opened and I stood face to face with a gorgeous set of hazel eyes: Leanne Armstrong. She wasn't wearing a whole lot, a pair of pale green bikini panties with lace in the front and a T-shirt that was too small for her torso.

"John Denson!" she squealed and stepped back, arms outstretched.

Well, I'll take on a warm form any day. I gave her a great big hug. "Same old John," she said.

I stepped back, held her with a hand on each shoulder, and took another look. Her T-shirt had "Maui Wowie!" written across the front. "But I gotta admit, you're a whole lot different."

"You were my first love, my very first. You don't know that but it's true. I thought you were sooooo handsome!" She grinned.

"I'm not any longer?"

"Oh yes, you are. You still are."

"Handsome John. Come a calling." I was having fun.

So was she. "A woman always wonders what he would have been like, you know. I know I always have." She put her hands on top of her head, laced her fingers, and took a deep breath. "Well?"

"Well, what?"

"You hardly glanced at me, stupid. How did I turn out? What do you think?"

I cleared my throat. "Let's see it all, gal. Your dad always wondered why I spent all my time worrying about jump shots."

She grinned. "You don't worry about jump shots anymore?"

"Oh, no. No, I haven't thought about jump shots for years."

Leanne put her hands on her waist, turned, and cocked her hips to one side. "Yes?"

"Yes."

"Then follow me, Mr. John Denson. We'll talk, then we'll play. Now's my chance after all these years. I'm not gonna be modest."

"Lead on," I said.

I followed her little rump, which had two marvelous little dimples above the top of her panties. I whacked my head on a Boston fern hanging from the ceiling before we got to the kitchen.

"You get high?"

"I get high," I said.

She got a plastic bag of dope from a cigar box that had once held rum-soaked Crooks and dumped some buds onto a round, lacquered tray with high sides and stylized Asian flowers in the middle. She separated seeds with a matchbook cover while I cased the room, trying to pretend I couldn't see her nipples through the T-shirt.

The kitchen had a white refrigerator that dated from the 1950s, when the designs were bloated and ugly. The linoleum tile on the floor was cracked with age and the corners were curled. The counters were piled high with dirty dishes.

There were two high wooden stools in front of an ancient gas stove: one for her, one for me.

She loaded a red plastic bong and gave it to me. "Matches or a lighter."

"I'm a match man," I said.

"Me too. I always burn my thumb with a lighter."

I took a hit and passed it back. "Nice place you have here," I said. It was a stupid comment but I didn't know what else to say. I guess I could have started with the weather.

"It's the shits is what it is. The art's mostly Larry's. He didn't show up tonight. It's true, what I said. I had a thing about you when I was a little girl. Call it what you want, infatuation, whatever, I don't care. You were special to me. Does that surprise you?"

"I don't think I ever gave it much thought."

She faked looking hurt, then smiled. "No reason why you should, I guess. But times have changed, don't you think? I've lived with three men and had two abortions. Here." She passed me the bong.

"Do you think it's oedipal or something, me wanting to be laid by you. I've fucked over fifty men, do you believe that?" She filled the bowl of the bong for herself. "They all want it, you know. You too. I figured what the hell?" She took another wad of marijuana buds from the plastic bag.

"Want me to sort?"

"Sure," she said.

I sorted while she removed her T-shirt. "Good dope," I said.

"Humboldt County. What do you think?"

"Beautiful." I meant it.

"Why thank you. Now are you gonna tell me what you're doing here in the middle of the night."

"I'm a detective here in Seattle, Leanne. A private investigator."

That startled her slightly. She shifted on her stool. "A private eye? Like in the movies?"

I laughed. "It's not exactly like in the movies but that's what I do."

"Really? I thought you were an intelligence agent or newspaper reporter or something."

"I was both of those at one time or another. I'm on my own now." I could hardly think. I was wondering when the panties would come down. "Your sister sent me after you. She's worried."

Leanne Armstrong began playing with the dope on the lacquered tray. "Jerry Hammond sent you after me."

"Well, maybe a little both. She's worried. He wants you."

"Hammond," she said. She loaded the bong again. "Three or four hits of this and we'll be whacked out of our skulls."

I shrugged. "What the hell."

"So what was Jerry's pitch?" She took a hit and waited.

"He said he's worried about you, but that's bullshit. He's about to score with a piece of art and you're trying to pull a scam."

"You are a detective, John Denson."

"He wants me to call him as soon as I find you."

"I'll bet he does."

I felt the warmth of the pot wash across my face. "My bet is you're working with amateurs and Hammond'll chop you up."

She grinned. "Jerry Hammond doesn't know where the hell we are, honey. You ever made it on a water bed?"

"I've made it on a water bed."

"We can talk there." The panties came down.

I followed. "We'll talk there."

"Look, do me a favor, will you? Don't call Hammond. I'll get in touch with Linda, you have my word on that. But leave Hammond out of it."

We slipped onto the bed together and it was there where I told Leanne what had happened to her sister in Sandy Johnson's bar.

I felt her body stiffen in my arms. "That son of a bitch," she said bitterly.

I said nothing. I could feel her breathing against my shoulder.

"That's all he said?"

"Who?"

"Jerry." She couldn't make up her mind how much she should reveal.

I took a long shot. "How about your friend, Sally?"

"What about her?"

"You don't read the newspapers."

"Haven't been."

"She was trying to pose as a stripper in Cayuse. She got her throat cut a few minutes after she told me you were up here in trouble."

"I want you to forget you found me."

"I find people, Leanne. That's my job. You're found. I have to tell your sister, at least."

"You tell Jerry and you'll do both my sister and me more harm than good."

She slipped her arms around me and held me as tightly as she could. "It's my fault," she said. "I want to tell you how it all happened but I can't. I can't erase what's already happened. It's past. Done."

"Yes, I guess it is."

Leanne suddenly slipped out of bed and went into the bathroom where I heard her blow her nose.

"Remind me some day to tell you about Sally," she said when she returned.

"My guess is that she was with you, watching Hammond while you ripped him off. The scam's now, this week."

"Nice try, John."

She had hesitated. She was lying.

83

"Maybe I'll tell you about her brother, Tony. And Jimmy Petrick."

A herring. "I'd like that," I said.

"Nobody ever had a better friend than Sally."

"I can believe that."

"Nobody."

"I know."

She began moving against me and her warmth was lovely. When I slipped into her she began working herself with her hand. Her fingernails dug into me as I moved in and out. It was the most erotic experience of my life.

When I woke up the next morning, Leanne was gone. So was the yellow Porsche that had been parked in the driveway the night before.

Eight

I FELT GOOD AS HELL when I stepped out into the slight breeze coming off the Sound. I was glad I'd given Pamela Yew the slip. I'd had a nice night with Leanne and found out she was out to relieve Jerry Hammond of whatever it was Pamela Yew was after. All I had to do was find Leanne again and stay with her. I had the license number of the Porsche. I was two steps up on Pamela.

Then I saw the BMW. Pamela Yew was reading a newspaper, which she folded carefully and put down. She took a sip of coffee from a paper cup and grinned. "I take it you had a lovely night, Mr. Denson. You better take all the free stuff you can get because your little bet with me is gonna cost."

I looked back at the apartment. "She wasn't bad. Maybe I could have her talk to you before you pay up."

"Oh, a little acrobat, eh? I must say she's a pretty thing, if you like 'em young."

I shrugged. "Younger, older. How did you get here?"

She looked surprised. "In this here BMW, love, how else? I followed you here."

"Well, you're here. That's nice."

"And what did all your sweating get you, Mr. Denson? Did you learn anything? About the case, I mean."

I couldn't help but laugh at that. "You gotta lot of gall, Ms. Yew. Try to hustle a man out of a painting worth fifty K then expect him to help you win the bet."

"You mean you're not going to help me?" She looked surprised.

"I don't reckon as how, ma'am. Which reminds me, why are you here drinking coffee out of a paper cup instead of tailing the girl?"

Pamela shrugged. "Because I ran a red light following her and was tagged by one Sergeant John Beckham of the Seattle Police. It'll cost me twenty-five bucks."

I couldn't help but laugh. "Twenty-five bucks?"

She nodded yes. "Do I buy breakfast or do you?"

"I'll buy this morning, what with your ticket and all. Tomorrow's your turn."

"Done. You can tell me all about Leanne. I mean, how was it? Did she wiggle her behind with great passion and all that?"

I closed my eyes. "Let's eat breakfast."

"Sure. You drive, Mr. Denson, I'll follow."

There was a cafe named the Fat City six blocks away. It didn't make any difference to Pamela Yew if I had slept with Leanne Armstrong but she liked to tease me. "Old bed 'em down John," she said, when the waitress brought her omelette. A half hour later we went our separate ways, she in her BMW, me in my Fiat.

I suspected Pamela Yew had her own idea of how to catch up with Leanne Armstrong. I took a turn south on I-5 to make sure I lost her for good, then reversed myself and drove to the art department at the University of Washington. I was in no hurry. I watched some potters and weavers at work before I asked for the location of the painting and drawing studios. The professor there was a lady named Virginia Mills. I remembered her name from a display at the Seattle Center maybe six months earlier. She painted little fat people.

It was the first day of spring semester at the university. When I stepped into the drawing studio there was a model up front going through some thirty-second sets. She was a tall girl with strong hips and small breasts. She had a slim waist and small, fragile shoulders. There was a strong light, set high and to her left, that produced some good highlights and shadows. Dramatic stuff. The model knew her business and took advantage of the light with some violent twists of her spine and stomach. The students had all the drama they could possibly want.

Virginia Mills came up to my side. I vaguely remembered her from a photograph at the center. She was perhaps fifty, with a husky figure under a brown dress. It looked like she had worn the same dress all week. She had a pleasant, intelligent face. It was obvious her students thought highly of her.

"A good student shouldn't have any trouble with a model like that."

"Mmmm," she said and nodded toward the model. The model stood on her toes, feet together, back to the students, and twisted her torso sharply to one side.

"What can I do for you?" she asked and dug casually at one armpit.

I felt in a goofy mood. "I'm a private investigator and I'm looking for the models you use for your paintings of fat people fucking."

She laughed. "At least you remembered them, didn't you, Mr.—"

"John Denson, and I was just kidding."

"How I do it, see, is squint my eyes when I paint. Sometimes when my lids get tired I put a rubber band around my head. The only problem there is headaches." She felt as goofy as me. She was a fun lady. She had smile lines on her face.

"Do you draw?" she asked.

I can tell you, that was flattering. "I once thought I wanted to be an artist but I didn't think there was any future in it. The truth is, I probably didn't want people to think I was a fag."

Professor Mills grinned at that.

"But that's not why I'm here. I'm looking for a girl named Leanne Armstrong, who is supposed to have earned extra money posing for art students."

"And?"

"And she's been missing for six months. Her twin sister is

87

worried." The model was on her side now in a classic pose in which the power of her hips was set in counterpoint to a soft slackness of stomach.

"Yes, I know Leanne. She worked for the department on and off last year. She had a good figure and wasn't a bad model. Is she in any kind of trouble?"

"Not that I know of. When was the last time you saw her?"

"She hasn't worked here in months."

"Are there any places around here where she might find work as a model?"

Professor Mills gave me the address of a Unitarian church. "They have several life drawing classes there; the models are paid according to enrollment. It's hard to get into studio classes here and a lot of students go there. They have fairly good instructors. They want models who know what they're doing. My husband has modeled there. They won't hire beginners."

"Can you remember anybody who might have been her friend?"

"No, I wouldn't be able to help you there."

"How about an artist named Larry?"

She looked at me like I was a trifle touched. "You have to be kidding, Mr. Denson. With all the students who come through here? I've had dozens of Larrys."

"It doesn't hurt to ask, I guess."

The model offered a profile now, with her back turned forward, shoulders down, and her rump turned towards the light.

"Just a few lines, well chosen, will do just nicely," Professor Mills told her students.

"What will they do?" I asked.

She shook her head. "The drama here is in her spine and hips."

"Will they pick up on that?"

She shrugged. "Some of them. Others will concentrate on the other as though that's all a woman is. They'll miss the power and beauty of a talented model, but what can I do? Is there anything else I can help you with? If there is anything I can do for Leanne, just let me know."

"Thanks much," I said.

"Say hello to Pamela for me will you?"

"Huh?" I did a double take.

Virginia Mills burst out laughing. "Pamela Yew and I are old friends. I selected one of her paintings for a show here last year."

"Why did you put me through this routine?"

"She thought it would be a little fun. It was. That's straight about the Unitarian church, though; Pamela asked me not to lie."

"Did she tell you about our bet?"

"An original Eakins! Heavens yes, she told me about the bet. I envy her."

"I can tell you things are not gonna end with you and all her friends admiring my Eakins in her living room."

"Oh?" She looked surprised. "How, exactly, do you think it will end, Mr. Denson?"

"With a tremor and a sigh, Professor Mills. With your friend Ms. Yew running the spectrum from violet to vermillion."

"Ohh, you are confident!"

"I'm gonna win."

She smiled. "We'll see. My money's on Pamela."

I waved goodbye and drove to the Unitarian church. I was going to have to hustle. John Denson against the feminist establishment of Seattle. What chance did I have?

An earnest young lady at the church told me to come back at seven p.m. The life drawing classes were held at night, she said. I bought a hot dog smothered with chili for lunch and took a walk in the Seattle zoo. You can learn a lot by watching animals. Later on, I had a Greek salad in a small cafe near the university campus. I consumed a small bottle of retsina wine and ordered extra anchovies on my salad.

When I returned to the church I was more sure than ever about the omen. There was a yellow Porsche parked outside. The license number was right: it was Leanne's. The Porsche was locked. The registration was strapped to the steering column at an angle that made it impossible to read. I went inside.

I didn't find Leanne right off. I found, instead, a fat man displaying his obese figure on a cotton carpet on the floor. He stared idly at the ceiling.

"Can I help you?"

I turned to face the instructor. She was younger than Professor Mills. "You like fat men?" she asked.

I gave her a look. Did I look like someone who likes fat men?

Pamela Yew stepped out of the shadows behind the instructor. "Well, hello, Mr. Denson."

"Are you going to invite the city of Seattle over to see your Eakins?"

Pamela smiled. "No, not everybody, love. Your friend Leanne's in the dressing room. She'll be out in a minute."

I heard the roar of an automobile engine outside the church. Pamela Yew looked at me.

"I think we've been had," I said.

"What do you mean 'we,' Mr. Macho? I was doing okay until you blundered along."

"I didn't see her give you a sisterly hug before she took off."

"Well, why don't you do something?"

"Me? She was spooked before I got here."

"She was *not.*"

I didn't answer. I was running to my Fiat to see if I could catch a tail light in the distance. I couldn't.

Nine

I RETURNED TO LEANNE'S apartment the next morning. It was empty; she'd split. Then I drove over to the office of the registrar at the University of Washington. I had given up worrying about Pamela. I had to hustle if I had a chance at the bet.

When I got to the registrar's office I was confronted with a familiar little sign on the wall that said no student's records would be released to outsiders unless the student gave his or her consent, in writing. There was a pile of orange forms that were used for the student's okay.

There were ways to get around that. I picked a clerk in her late twenties as the best bet. Any younger than that you take a chance on a political ideologue. Much older and you take a chance on a professional bureaucrat. The latter is impressed only by posted regulations, never position or authority. They always, always ask questions.

I picked my pigeon and stepped up to the window.

"My name is Mr. Denson of Army Intelligence. I'm doing a routine background check on a student here named Larry Fowler. Mr. Fowler is being considered for a position of trust and responsibility by the United States government."

I flashed my private investigator's license in front of her too fast to see. I looked grave and important.

"Yes, sir." She blinked once, had nice eyes.

"I'd like to see his records, please."

"Where's Bill Copple?"

I was in luck. This man Copple obviously knew the ways of clerks. Bless him. "He's on leave this week, didn't he tell you? I'm up from San Francisco on TDY."

"He didn't tell me." She went to get the records of Larry Fowler. No luck. He had never been registered at the University of Washington.

"Thanks much," I said. I turned to leave when I remembered someone else. "Oh, yes. I almost forgot," I said. "I have another name to check; student name of Sally Whipple."

This time I scored.

My clerk returned with file in hand. "What is it you want to know?" She made a point of not handing over the folder. The game varied. In this version I had to ask my questions; I couldn't browse.

"Her current status," I said. That should cover everything.

She studied the file. "You people probably have everything that's here. She was a graduate assistant in modern dance. Dropped out a few weeks ago. There's a notation says she didn't say why. Just didn't show up. Beautiful girl, judging from her picture."

Leanne had said she had studied literature before she studied art. She hadn't said exactly what kind of art.

"I have one other check to run, young woman name of Leanne Armstrong."

The clerk ran a check and came up with another folder. "Yes, Ms. Armstrong received a B.A. in American literature and was accepted into the M.A. program in art history as an assistant to poor Dr. Palmer."

"Poor Dr. Palmer?"

The clerk looked surprised. "Yes. Dr. Eric Palmer. He was murdered last summer on his way to an art reception."

I took a random note to meet my cover. "Can you tell me Dr. Palmer's specialty?"

She looked even more surprised. "Why, Asian art. He was said to be tops in his field."

Two other colleges in town, Seattle University and Seattle Pacific, were private colleges and didn't have any civil-rights hangups. The clerks there checked and gave me my no on Larry Fowler right off. So did the area's junior colleges.

I checked and there was no Lawrence or Larry Fowlers among the twenty-seven Fowlers listed in the Seattle telephone directory. The information operator couldn't help either. So I bought a six-pack of San Miguel dark and settled down by the phone in my room to start with Fowler, Aaron, and work my way to Fowler, Wilma. Between busy signals, no answers and call backs, that took half my six-pack and two hours of my time. No luck. Non-student Larry Fowler was apparently not a local boy.

It had rained that morning, turning the snow to slush, but now it was snowing again so I bought a copy of the Seattle *Star* with the idea of relaxing and watching the snow. It doesn't often snow in Seattle. This was an unusual winter. I didn't relax very long. On my way to the sports section I happened across a two-paragraph item on the death of one Lawrence R. Fowler, of a local address, who was found stabbed to death in downtown Seattle.

I checked with my answering service to see how much paying business had piled up. Emma reported the usual nags, the stuff with which I pay my rent. But I wanted to see the Leanne Armstrong business through to the end.

I got into my Fiat and headed for the *Star*. I had two good friends there, Charley Powell, the city editor, and a reporter named Bob Sander. If neither of them were in I would go drink somewhere, maybe at Pig's Alley. Powell was there, hunkered over his desk reading press releases.

"What a bunch of shit!" he said. He swept a pile of half-truth into a waste basket. "Assholes," he said. Tiny beads of sweat had formed on the front of his balding head. "Denson, you jerk, where have you been?"

I shrugged. "Rescuing damsels, Charley. Pursuing justice. Fighting the good fight."

He grinned. "Sitting on your butt, eh?"

"No, as a matter of fact I had a client for a couple of days there." I told him about Pamela Yew and our bet.

Powell giggled. "You don't suppose I could wangle an invite to the payoff, do you? I'd bring along a photographer and we could run a picture spread for the Sunday paper. Ms. Pamela Yew and her handsome Eakins. I'd write the cutlines myself."

"You might talk her into selling tickets. She's from San Francisco but it seems like she's pals with every female artist in Seattle. They'll all be there, why not you?"

Powell shook his head. "How can I help?"

"Is Bob Sander in? I need some help with the cops but I think I've been overusing my contact down there."

"Sander wangled a junket to Alaska. You can talk to our new cops man if you want. I don't think he has brains enough to pour piss out of a boot with the directions on the heel but he gets the job done."

"A guy named Phillips had an item about a body in this afternoon's rag. I'm trying to trace the stiff."

"That's the guy, up from the Oakland *Tribune*. But I gotta warn you, brace yourself for Phillips."

Across the city room came the cops man. He was middle-aged, with a paunch that hung over his belt. He had eyes that squinted and a lop-sided grin that exposed ugly teeth. I could have lit his breath with a cigarette lighter.

Power introduced us. "John Denson, Wayne Phillips. He ain't James Reston but so far he's done a job, drunk as he is."

We shook hands. Phillips laughed soundlessly. He wobbled slightly and hung onto the edge of Powell's desk. A cigarette was stuck to his lower lip; the smoke drifted up past his watery, permanently squinted eyes.

"Ain't much happened today. Bastards are off their feed out there. No one raped. No one burned alive. A stiff or two but nothing good."

"Maybe you can help Denson here. What was the name of that dead man, John?"

"The papers say Lawrence R. Fowler," I said.

94

Powell looked at Phillips. "Do you still have the dope on that?"

Phillips looked at me through squinty eyes. Powell had asked him a dumb question. Of course he had the dope on Fowler. He was a professional. "Whatcha need?"

"An address on the guy."

He flipped through a small green notebook. "Didn't I have that in the story?"

"You said he lived in the 600 block of Wilder Avenue."

He had done that to avoid possible mixups and lawsuits. "Oh," he said. He gave me the full address.

"One more thing," I said. "Do you guys suppose I could check a couple of names in your morgue."

"Library," Phillips corrected me. "You call that place a morgue and the old broad up there'll cut your tongue out."

"Go with him, Wayne," Powell said.

Phillips went with me. "Tell me whatcha want before we get there."

"I want you to check the names Tony Whipple and Jimmy Petrick for about two years back."

Phillips obliged and hung on the counter to steady himself while we waited. I thought I could drink and work but I was penny ante compared to Phillips. The girl came back with two small clips. Whipple and Petrick had their throats cut the same day in two separate locations in Seattle the previous summer. Phillips studied the clips over my shoulder.

"Well, thanks, Wayne," I said and turned to leave.

Phillips put a hand on my shoulder. "In Seattle, two guys knifed the same day is a whole lotta guys knifed in one day. I can't imagine you don't remember reading about it."

"I remember."

"Well, the deal is, see, Charley doesn't let something like that die. He doesn't like the idea of being a city editor in a bush league city. Big league cities've got gangsters; people cut other people's throats."

"Charley wants gangsters."

Phillips nodded his head. "He wants gangsters and he's a

goddam nag about it. He's like a frigging elephant, never forgets."

I understood what he was saying. "I know what you mean."

"He know what you're onto?"

"No."

"What else do you know?"

"Bits and pieces."

"You scratch backs?"

"Sure," I said.

"Now you don't mention a word of this to Powell. He even has a hint there's something this big going on in town he'll hound my ass to have it in two hours. Things don't work that way. You know that?"

"I know that," I said. I knew what he was up against.

"Best for me if Charley thinks I got it all on my own. What he doesn't know won't hurt him. What I want to know is what's in this for you?"

I wanted to ask him just what it was that I was after but I didn't dare risk my ignorance. I'd have to ease it out of him bit by bit. "The girl Leanne Armstrong used to be my neighbor in Cayuse. I used to hunt geese with her old man."

Phillips looked at me like I was nuts. "Gal got her throat cut nosing around there. Just a few days ago. You know her?"

"Sally Whipple. A little."

"You want to compare notes now?" he said.

"Leanne Armstrong's trying to hustle Jerry Hammond. I know the car she's driving and enough details to run her to ground."

The squinty eyes studied me. "It's coming out of Canada. Keep in touch. And mum's the word with Charley."

"Mum's the word," I said. I gave him the license number of the Porsche to check out with the cops. He said he would. Canada. Thing mineral was going to be smuggled.

"Hey, you two, what the hell's going on over there?" Charley Powell yelled from the city desk.

"Talking about getting laid, Charley. You ever been laid?"

"Crap," Powell muttered. He returned to the press releases piled on his desk. I headed for my Fiat.

96

I didn't expect anybody to be home at the Wilder Avenue address Phillips had given me. I was surprised. It was an old brick apartment building. I walked up two flights of stairs, took a right, and lo, there was the door with the right number on it.

It was open.

Inside there was a young man drinking beer and reading a Masked Marvel comic book. From the clutter inside it looked like he was packing. There were a couple of suitcases on the couch.

I rapped twice on the door jamb.

He looked up. He had pale blue eyes, a scraggy blond mustache that needed fertilizer, and a large nose. There was a ripe pimple on the end of the nose. He put down the comic book and placed one hand very carefully under a towel on an end table by his chair. The towel had been lifted from the Mayflower Hotel.

"You can learn a lot from comics, do you know that?" he asked. He was content to leave me standing in the hall.

What the hell, I can't expect everybody to love me. "Do you know a guy named Larry Fowler?"

"Knew him. Got his throat cut with a toadstabber yesterday. Whoring around. I did book reports on classic comics in high school."

"Mind if I come in?"

"What do you want?"

"I'm trying to find a girlfriend of Larry's," I said. There was a revolver under the towel.

"What's her name?"

"Leanne Armstrong, a pretty little blonde."

He thought about that for a moment. "Don't know her," he said. He was lying. His hand trembled under the towel.

"Mind if I ask you some questions anyway?"

"I mind but it looks like you're going to ask them anyway, so sit. You a cop?"

I sat on a worn-out sofa next to the suitcases and looked at the posters on the walls. Naked ladies and such. "What can you tell me about Larry Fowler?"

"I said who are you, anyway?"

"My name is John Denson. I'm a private investigator. Who are you?"

"Lewis Cooper."

"Well, Lewis Cooper, how long did you live with Fowler?"

"Couple years, for what it's worth." Cooper poured himself another mug of beer from a quart bottle. The mug had been lifted from a bar. "Treble Tripe" the decal said.

"Can you give me any help at all in finding Leanne Armstrong?"

"I told you already, I don't know any chick by that name."

"How about friends of Fowler's who might have known her?"

"I don't know who he ran around with. I met him at a party one night. We became friends. We shared an apartment to save money. I don't know where he was from or what he did before I met him. He didn't tell me and it wasn't any of my business."

"You can't give me any help, then?"

"I'm afraid not."

"How did he feed his face?"

"He was an artist, you know. He picked up a little bread here, a little there. Women liked him."

"What women?"

"How the hell should I know? All I know is, he was getting his. He wasn't hurting."

"You're telling me you lived with the guy for two years and that's all you know about him?"

"That's it, bud. That's just what I'm telling you. I'm telling you he wasn't a half-bad guy. He was my friend and he's dead. Some son of a bitch took him out. What I want to know is why? He never hurt anybody. He never hurt anybody and he's dead. All I know is I got a call from the cops. I went down to the morgue and it was him. Dead. A guy never hurt anybody. The way I see it, what he did was his business. You're not a cop; I don't owe you anything."

I pulled out my picture of Linda Hammond. "This is Leanne Armstrong's identical twin. Are you sure you haven't seen her around?"

98

Cooper studied the photograph. "Wish I had. Not a bad-looking piece."

"Thanks anyway," I said. "Have a nice trip to Canada."

"Canada? Canada sucks."

He was a liar. "Thanks, anyway," I said.

I notice a couple of "Treble Tripe" coasters on a coffee table.

"What's the Treble Tripe?"

"Huh?"

"The Treble Tripe?"

"A joint with a band," he said.

"Thanks again," I said and left.

When I got back to the street again I found my car had a flat tire. The spare was flat too. I rolled both of them to a Shell station on the corner.

I got my tire fixed and when I pulled onto the street there was Pamela Yew. She must have spotted Phillips's article in the *Star* and traced the address through the morgue. I pulled over to the side of the road and waved to her. She pulled alongside my Fiat and rolled down the window on the passenger's side of her BMW.

"You want a word with me, Mr. Denson?" she asked.

"The guy in there's name is Lewis Cooper. He lived with Fowler for two years. He's scared half to death and won't say a thing."

"Oh?"

"He also has a pistol with him. You want to come with me to a place called the Treble Tripe? There might be something in it."

She shook her head. "No, Mr. Denson, I'll ask my own questions. You go on ahead."

I shrugged. "Suit yourself but take care."

"Thank you, Mr. Denson."

"I want you in one piece for my payoff."

She pulled a U-turn in the street and went back to Cooper's apartment. I headed for the Treble Tripe.

The Treble Tripe was in the college community near the University of Washington campus. It was about four blocks off the main drag of book shops, record shops, taverns, clothing shops and fast-food joints. The Tripe was a popular place—from which high-pitched wails tortured the cold night air as I approached. It was a certain electronic madness born of San Francisco and diluted over the years to five percent of its former acidity by nineteen-year-old entrepreneurs who know how to sell tapes and records to other nineteen-year-olds.

A piece of cardboard taped to the door identified the source of the wailing: Mellow Boys and the Kind Lady. The sign said they came direct from the planet Mars.

I glanced around. It was all noise and confusion, sound and fury. I gave up on looking for someone who might have known Larry Fowler and found a place to sit. An overweight girl who looked like a refugee from the peace movement and who called herself a "Klamath" offered me a joint. I guess I took one too many tokes. By the time I came out of my own personal fog, I realized that an hour or so had passed. I said goodbye to the Klamath and fought my way back through the bodies blocking the door.

When I got outside I remembered that, at least for me, driving and dope don't mix. I decided to walk the half-mile or so to Larry Fowler and Lewis Cooper's apartment to clear my head, maybe check in with Pamela if she was still staking things out, and get back to my car after I'd brought my brain waves back to normal.

I was about fifteen yards from Lewis Cooper's apartment when its front door opened; a girl stepped out and began trotting off through the rain. I saw her clearly under the high-crime street light: Leanne Armstrong.

I hadn't considered that she might have company. Someone stepped out of the shadows behind her and whacked me over the head. I hit the sidewalk on my knees.

I felt warm blood sliding down the side of my temple and looked up to see Pamela Yew.

"Dammit, John, I've been watching this place all night. Just when I get a little action you have to blunder along and get thumped on the head."

"Go ahead, tail them. I'll be all right."

"You know I can't do that."

"I'm sorry. You were one up on me; I messed it up for you."

"Oh, that's okay." She helped me to my feet and turned my head to the light so she could see my cut. "You'll probably have a headache but you'll be all right."

"Listen, do me a favor, will you. Give me your phone number so I can get in touch with you if I have to. I don't like the cast of this plot. One of us might need the other's help."

"You know what it is you're after yet?"

I shook my head no.

She grinned. "I didn't think so." She gave me her number.

Ten

THE LATE LEWIS COOPER, reader of Captain Marvel comic books, was on the radio the next morning. Cooper had his throat cut just like his buddy, Larry Fowler. Early in the morning, the police said. That would have been about the time I spotted Leanne coming out of the building and got whacked on the head. Pamela Yew was watching the front door from across the street so the murderer must have used another entrance.

It must have been the murderer who gave me my headache.

I no sooner laid the paper down than Wayne Phillips called. "Read the old rag this morning, Denson?"

"I read it."

"Charley's getting anxious about gangsters again. He sees us exposing the whole thing, see, winning big awards for service to the city of Seattle, all that." He coughed a smoker's hack.

"You take care of Charley; I'll keep hustling out here. I'll keep in touch."

"You better hustle awful damn fast, man."

"Later, Wayne, I'll keep in touch." I hung up and got Pamela Yew on the phone.

She seemed in good spirits. "Good morning, Mr. Denson; you've been listening to the radio, I'll bet."

"That's it," I said. "I think we should talk things over."

"You're thinking we should work more closely together."

"For our own protection. But we continue the competition."

She laughed. "I agree, the competition must continue. I have too many friends worked up over the bet. They'll be disappointed if I let them down."

"What do you say we meet at Pig's Alley, a tavern just off Pike's Market."

"I've never been there but I'll find it; I like Pike's."

"In an hour, say."

"See you then."

We hung up.

The walk from my apartment felt good. It was a trifle cold outside but not enough to stop a good walker. I had some time so I hit Pike's Market before the Pig's. Pike's was one of the best big-city fish and vegetable markets I'd ever seen. The big reason was the vegetables. The fish too. I love to eat raw cauliflower and smoked fish. There's something exceptionally lovely about the produce section of supermarkets. You admire a water colorist for his ability to suggest a cow in the distance with a squiggle of color. Or for his ability to lay out a juniper with a twist of Hooker's green. But I've yet to see an artist who could do justice to a bin full of cabbage.

I was a familiar face to the vendors at Pike's. For them an attractive display was a way to sell asparagus or tomatoes. But it was different for me—a matter of esthetics—and they knew it. They watched me carefully when I examined their displays, looking for a hint or clue to my reaction. I was their jurist, a man of taste in matters of vegetable display.

The merchants at Pike's don't use cellophane, a sign of esthetic purity. A good way to ruin a display of vegetables is to cover everything in cellophane; it destroys the way the light reflects off the texture of the vegetables and fruit. Plums are especially subtle in that regard. Fish display well also, but not red meat; there's precious little difference between a pork chop and a rib eye steak. But place a slab of rich red Chinook alongside some cod, maybe, or sole and you have something else. The fish men watched me also but they knew I was really a vegetable man. They didn't care. They had pride. A vegetable man was better than nothing at all.

"Your smelt look fantastic today, just lovely, Bill."

You don't know what a comment like that can do for a fish man. What difference does it make if you can't get your mind off avocados, leeks, beets, and turnips?

Anyway, I looked at the vegetables while I waited for Pamela Yew. There wasn't much to be found in the way of vegetables, it being the middle of winter. So I hung around the fish counters admiring snapper and squid. It was a cold day at Pike's: customers were scarce. For a while there was just me and a guy in a gray overcoat who spent a lot of time staring at greens. I guess every man to his taste. Greens are good to eat but there's not much you can do with them on a vegetable counter.

He stared at greens. Queer taste.

I bought a small head of overpriced cauliflower and a chunk of even more overpriced smoked salmon and headed for Pig's Alley to wait for Pamela.

The Pig's was not a classy place to drink. I liked it because it overlooked some old warehouses and Puget Sound. The warehouses had windows broken in. Seagulls floated in the salty air above the Sound. There was an empty lot overgrown with weeds and a railroad track that wasn't used anymore. One afternoon I drank beer and watched two girls about eighteen years old get into a fight in the tall weeds. There was no one else there, just the two of them. They went at one another with fingernails while I watched from above, drinking draught beer and eating popcorn. Pretty soon one got up and ran off. The other lay in the sun weeping. I didn't want her to be crying; for no reason I began to water up also.

Old men drank at the Pig's because the beer was cheap. So did young men for the same reason.

I saved my cauliflower and salmon to share with Pamela. After awhile a black girl came in. She wasn't selling newspapers.

She was wearing a large red wig that had the apparent consistency of a Brillo pad. She wore purple trousers that were a second skin and a bright green blouse that barely restrained

104

her large breasts. That wasn't helped by the fact that the top three buttons were undone. She walked confidently in and pivoted on cork-soled platform shoes, inviting us to admire her powerful thighs and enormous rear. She did a couple of sample bumps and grinds with her hips and looked at the man at the other table, at me, and at the three men sitting at the bar. All of us looked back with respect at the audacity of her outfit but none of us gave her the response she was looking for. I thought it strange that one guy at the bar ignored her. His beer was obviously more interesting. You'd have to be a eunuch to do that. The black girl thought that was odd too. She looked at him and gave us a shrug. Then she grinned and silently mouthed "queer" behind his back. "You don't know what you're missing, honey," she said aloud. She gave us a big grin and a wink, patted herself on the butt and went about her appointed rounds.

She passed Pamela Yew coming in.

"Hello, Mr. Denson. You're looking fit this morning. Interesting clientele at your bar."

I broke off some cauliflower and salmon for her. "I want you to look at that guy sitting at the bar and tell me what's wrong."

"Am I to be your Watson, Sherlock?"

I shrugged. "Whatever."

She studied the man carefully. "Well, he's overdressed for this place. He looks self-conscious. He's drinking Michelob. This is an Olympia and Rainier place."

"Well done. There's more. I was out in the market admiring vegetables before I came in here to wait for you. That guy was out there admiring mustard greens."

"So?"

"A guy like that doesn't eat mustard green. He eats asparagus. Besides that they're ugly, Ms. Yew. I'm surprised at you! An artist, and all."

She looked impressed. "Continue, Holmes, by all means."

"Well, there was that hooker that you passed on your way in. She came in and gave us a little pass in review, her idea of come hither. The guy at the bar didn't turn to watch, which is harmless enough. And there's the overcoat."

105

"Overcoat?"

"He was wearing a gray overcoat in Pike's. Now he doesn't have an overcoat. No overcoat and he wants to make sure we see his back, not his face. Now there's no overcoat on the rack. What did he do with it? What do you suppose became of his overcoat?"

"I don't know."

"He stashed it with a vegetable man in the market along with five bucks. Said he'd pick it up in a few minutes."

"Why would he do that?"

I shrugged. "I can't imagine it has anything to do with us, Ms. Yew, but I think we should go for a little walk and find out."

"But we just got here, Mr. Denson. Let's enjoy the view."

"Humor me. We'll probably be back in a few minutes."

"What's your suspicion?"

"I think that man at the bar is a cop of some kind. I think he's a rookie."

Pamela rolled her eyes and looked disgusted. "Oh, come on. Believe me, there's nothing about what I'm after that could possibly involve the government."

"What do you say we at least make sure? If he's tailing somebody else, no harm done."

She looked at the man at the bar again. "Okay, Mr. Denson, I'll humor you. What do we do?"

"First of all, we'll take a leisurely stroll through Pike's. I want you to keep an eye on him and tell me what you see."

She waved her hand in the direction of the door. "After you; gentlemen first."

We had gotten halfway down the main aisle of vegetable displays when Pamela reported on the man at the bar.

"He's back there, Mr. Denson, wearing a gray overcoat."

"Well, it's a crisp day. He'll need it. Would you like to go for a walk downtown, Pamela?"

"Sure." She was curious about the man in the overcoat and wondered what I had in mind.

"We'll walk for at least two blocks before we check. When

106

we do, you look, not me. Check the sidewalk across the street and maybe a block to our rear."

"What'll I find."

"Gray overcoat."

"Bull!"

"We'll see." We walked. Two blocks later I paused at a corner. "Time for your check, Ms. Yew. Be casual now."

She turned. "You're right, Mr. Denson, across the street and a block back."

"Doing what? Staring at a window display? I say sporting goods."

Pamela laughed. "Women's shop."

"Stay with me, gal. You'll learn a lot. We'll cross the street here but stay east. When we get to the other side he'll come across to our side. Want to bet on that?"

"I'm not so sure I do now." The light changed. We crossed.

"Well?" I asked.

"He moved over just like you said. What's going on?"

"Someone is working an elementary surveillance rotation on us, Ms. Yew. Your tax dollars once taught me how to do that. It's no big deal, but the idea is the rabbit isn't supposed to spot the foxes."

"Which we have."

"Indeed. Overcoat is perfectly awful. There'll be at least three of them. The trick now is to find the others without them knowing it."

Pamela Yew laughed. "I like this—adding to my skills. What do we do after we have them spotted?"

"If it's okay with you, I think we should have a little fun with them. Show 'em what a flaky detective and a smart broad can do."

"I'm game. Only don't call me a broad."

I took her by the elbow and steered her through a jaywalk. On the other side I walked briskly up a lateral street. Pamela had to hustle to keep up with me. I paused in front of a jewelry store window to watch the action behind me.

"See there, Ms. Yew." A man in a snappy green fedora began walking across the intersection with the yellow light against

107

him. "If Fedora's part of the rotation, both Overcoat and the man who took his place will be momentarily out of position. Makes it a bit hairy for them."

"Fedora has us all by himself."

"Ah, you're a quick learner." Fedora relaxed when he saw us dawdling. "They'll be getting their setup straight now. Lucky for them the streets were filled with people. Eye on Fedora now." I started walking again and spotted the third man. "The man with the big shoulders over there is the last one, Pamela."

"I think this is marvelous. How does it work?" Pamela was having fun.

"Simple enough, they rotate positions: forward, backwards, right or left, depending on which way we turn and how long we continue in one direction. The idea is never to have one man behind us for too long a time."

There was suddenly an added spring in Pamela's step. "What'll happen now?"

"We'll keep walking. In maybe three blocks Shoulders and Fedora will switch places. Overcoat will trail, either in the second spot behind us or across the street. He was too close to us at the Pig's and in Pike's for him to take the catbird seat directly behind us."

They made the switch in two blocks.

"I bet they think we're some kind of physical fitness nuts, Pamela. Shall we see what kind of stuff they're made of? We haven't done anything wrong; they need the practice."

"Certainly, Mr. Denson."

I headed for the terminal to the monorail.

Shoulders was in the catbird when we got to the terminal. I bought a *Newsweek* from a stand and watched the action while I pretended to browse through a paperback.

"This is fun, Mr. Denson. Just like the movies."

"Just like the movies. We're gonna irritate these gentlemen. Do I buy the monorail tickets or do you?"

"I'll buy."

"Then buy four."

Her eyebrows went up. "I think you just pulled one on me."

I shrugged. "We step inside the train and take the front seat,

108

the one nearest the front entrance. Either Fedora or Shoulders will buy a ticket and follow us inside. Just before the doors close we'll step back out onto the platform. Got that?"

"Got it."

We got on the train. Shoulders looked back at Fedora. Fedora nodded slightly. He was the honcho. Shoulders bought a ticket, came aboard and took a seat behind us.

"Now, Mr. Denson?" Pamela whispered.

"Now, love." We stepped back onto the platform. I looked back into the car. Shoulders stared at his feet. Eye contact is sin number one for a covert tail; he had to stay as the train left.

That left us with two: Overcoat—who had come close to being burned—and the boss man, Fedora. Fedora was in the catbird seat. Overcoat trailed.

"Nicely done, John. What do we do now?"

"Pretty soon one of them will have to make a phone call to relay instructions to Shoulders, who will call in once he reaches Seattle Center." There was a delicatessen across the street. "What do you say we have ourselves a hot dog and give the poor bastards a chance?"

"Sounds good."

It was too. The hot dogs had fresh sauerkraut and brown mustard. Overcoat, I saw, zipped into a bar to make his phone call. Big Shoulders would be joining them in a few minutes, having come from the Space Needle by cab. We took our time with our hot dogs. When we stepped outside, they were in their places.

"What do you think, Pamela, time for the monorail again?" I asked.

"Whatever you say. I'm along for the fun."

They couldn't risk either Overcoat or Shoulders on the monorail so it would be up to Fedora. Fedora was cocky; he thought he'd never get taken like Shoulders.

I leaned in and asked the pilot how long it would be before the monorail left for the Space Needle. He said two minutes. I motioned for Pamela to join me on a nearby bench.

"They saw us buy tickets just once. We used those when

we suckered Shoulders. We'll wait until the very second the monorail is due to leave, then step inside. Got that?"

Pamela laughed. "Got it." She snuck a look at Fedora.

Fedora hung back. He thought it was safe. I checked my watch; four seconds before the time was up I nudged Pamela in the ribs. We stepped quickly onto the monorail; the door slid shut. We were on our way.

"Fun, John Denson!"

"I'm sure Fedora doesn't think so. They'll have to bust their tails to beat us there by taxi. They'll have to leave one here in case we pull a reverse. That'll leave them shorthanded at the Center end."

"Why don't they just ask us what they want? We haven't broken any laws?"

"Pamela, Pamela, you should know by now the government never does anything the easy way when it can make things complicated."

"They're in place now, John."

"Shall we give them one last run?"

"Let's."

We strode briskly out of the Center and moved across a parking lot at a near trot. Overcoat was right after us. A construction outfit was in the process of destroying some old buildings; I ducked under a rope and pulled Pamela after me. We started moving in and out between Caterpillar tractors, earth movers and pickup trucks. Overcoat hung right in there. Just past the construction site I turned down a small side street. There was a working man's tavern on one side. Clyde's Bar & Grill, the sign said.

"What do you say we take a breather and leave them out there in the cold to think it over?"

"Whatever you say, Mr. Denson." Pamela looked back to see how Fedora had deployed his troops. We had beaten them around the corner.

"Quickly, Pamela." We stepped inside the front door of Clyde's. Inside was a bar and one row of wooden booths. There were two people in Clyde's: a fat bartender and a black man sitting under a yellow construction hat. Just before the men's room there was a door. I tried the door for the hell of it. The door opened into a broom closet. It had once been an entrance into a larger storeroom but someone had walled it off. And lo! The lock was still on the inside of the door, a sliding-bolt lock.

"Here, quickly."

Pamela joined me, looking puzzled.

I didn't give her a chance to say anything and pulled her into the closet and locked the door after us. It wasn't much of a closet; it was about the size of a coffin stood on end and contained a mop bucket with a wringer on top, several mops, assorted brushes hanging from hooks, a half-empty box of paper towels, and not much else. The place smelled of pine oil.

Pamela Yew and I found ourselves smashed up against one another, face to face. We could hardly breathe.

"This is nice," I whispered.

"Control yourself, Mr. Denson."

"You have a heartbeat, I can feel it."

"Of course I have a heartbeat."

"I was beginning to wonder, after you set the terms for our bet." I moved against the warmth of her torso. "Feeling randy," I whispered.

She tried to nudge me with her knees but could hardly move. "Damn you," she whispered back.

Someone tried the door to the closet. We could hear people talking. A man asked the bartender if anyone had come into his establishment. The bartender said yes, a man and a woman.

"That's all?" asked the man.

"I don't know, there may be someone back there on the toilet," said the bartender.

We could hear the man checking the toilet. "Nobody back here," he called to the front of the tavern. "Where'd they go?"

Somebody tried the closet door once again.

"That locks from the outside, genius," a second voice said.

Footsteps disappeared out the front of the tavern. "Where the hell did they go?" the first voice asked again.

I waited; I could feel Pamela breathing against me.

111

"Don't you think we can get out of here now, Casanova?" Pamela said softly.

"I wouldn't mind staying like this all afternoon."

Pamela Yew unbolted the door.

The bartender could hardly believe it when he saw us emerge from the back of his tavern. "Where did you two disappear to?"

"Had a little nooner behind the john there."

The bartender looked confused.

I looked outside. There was a phone booth across the street. Fedora was inside involved in an animated discussion on the phone. Overcoat and Shoulders were looking up and down the narrow street as though Pamela and I were going to miraculously reappear. It was a scene out of the silent movies.

"Shall we have some fun, Pamela?"

Pamela grinned. "Why not?"

I opened the door to Clyde's Bar & Grill and said, "Hey!"

"What?" Overcoat looked my way in disbelief.

"I said, 'Hey!' "

"Hey what?" Overcoat was clearly embarrassed at making a stupid reply. Later he would wonder why he couldn't have come up with something clever.

"Why don't you guys come on over and have a beer?" Pamela called.

"Atta girl," I said. "Better than Lauren Bacall."

"What?" Shoulders this time. He could hardly believe it. He pounded on the phone booth trying to get Fedora's attention.

"She said come on over and have a beer. We're sociable. We've had enough exercise."

They walked sullenly across the street, staring at the pavement and not saying anything. Pamela Yew, with an enormous grin, opened the door and they filed in one at a time, Fedora first, followed by Overcoat and Shoulders. Once inside they stood nervously, shuffling their feet.

"Nice little bar," said Shoulders.

"What'll we have, gents?" I said. "Couple of pitchers?"

Overcoat nodded his head yes.

"It's on me, gentlemen," Pamela said with a generous wave of her hand.

"No, no." Overcoat fumbled for his wallet. No woman was gonna buy his beer.

Too late, Pamela had paid. I collected the pitchers from the bartender. The three of them trailed after Pamela and me to a wooden booth. Shoulders brought the glasses; he was low man.

I poured the beer. Overcoat was still concerned at Pamela's having sprung for the pitchers.

"You fellows work very nicely together," Pamela said. Poor bastards. She was letting them have it.

"Hell of a day to be running around the streets of Seattle," I said. "Nip in the air. Good for the legs. Blows the fat out of your veins."

Fedora gave me a kiss-my-ass look. I thought I saw his jaw muscles grind for a second but I wasn't sure.

"Shall we start with introductions?" I offered.

Fedora shook his head no.

"But of course you already know who we are. Denson and Yew, master detectives."

"We know who you are," said Fedora.

"Can we help you with anything?" Pamela asked.

Fedora nodded his head yes. He clearly did not like Pamela Yew's participation. This was a man's game, like rugby or poker.

"Where did you learn that stuff?" asked Shoulders. He wasn't low after all. Overcoat was. The question was directed at me.

"What stuff?" I asked.

"Out there." He nodded toward the street and drank beer at the same time. He saw himself as Bogart, maybe. I could see Fedora wanted the answer too.

"The Bird," I said. "Peary."

"Holabird?" Overcoat said stupidly. That was like saying "that's where the president lives" after someone mentions the White House. He was both low and dumb. Next time I saw him he'd be in charge. The government's in the market for people like him. He tried to sneer but it came off like he had a fly on his lip.

"Listen, *we* invited *you* in here, friend," I said. "Where were you? Besides that, Ms. Yew here called the shots out there, not me."

Fedora started to smirk. But he had to watch it. If he had a sense of humor he wouldn't go far. The government regards laughter as a personal defect, like not brushing your teeth. Laughs are recorded on federal personnel forms, to be counted as dings come promotion time. Fedora had to be careful.

However, once Fedora laughed it was okay for the others, and Shoulders laughed too, although he didn't see anything very funny. Fedora was his supervisor. Fedora laughs, Shoulders laughs. That's the way it works. The president of the United States laughs at a bad joke and twenty-four hours later it's repeated to a postal clerk in Sparks, Nevada, who laughs dutifully.

Fedora spoke for the first time. "When did you go through?"

"Fall of '63," I said.

Shoulders perked up. Overcoat was still sullen. The fact that Pamela Yew was grinning at his discomfort didn't help matters.

"Say, did you know a guy named Bobby Dankers?" asked Shoulders.

"Knew him well. Helluva guy. Bobby Dankers could spot a rabbit in Yankee Stadium."

"Could he stay with you?" asked Fedora.

"In Times Square," I said.

Fedora bought two more pitchers, even though we hadn't finished the first round. "This one's on Sam," he said, referring to the good Uncle.

"If you guys are trying to get us drunk, forget it; Pamela never gets drunk."

"Thirsty," said Fedora.

"When did you spot me?" asked Overcoat. He was loosening up a little. Maybe being a jerk was getting tiresome.

"I wondered why you didn't case the hooker in Pig's Alley. And when you spent so much time staring at mustard greens in Pike's I thought you were a mental case. Greens taste good but they're as ugly as hell. You should have picked yellow squash—there's a vegetable. Then there was that on again, off again business with your overcoat."

Fedora leaned over the table to ask the next question. Overcoat gave him the floor.

"Why were you looking for a tail?"

"I wasn't. I just told you why Overcoat here stood out like a white sprinter at the Olympics."

"No, no. That isn't enough."

"That's the way it was."

Fedora retreated to think that one over.

"Where did you hide inside this joint?" asked Shoulders.

"Broom closet back there was once part of an entrance into storeroom. Door locks from the inside. Pamela and I were inside enjoying . . . what would you call it Pamela?"

"Disgusting closeness."

I shrugged. "Whatever. We could hear you guys crashing around out here like a trio of dinosaurs."

Fedora grinned. "Well, there's no harm done, I guess."

"No harm done if we stayed lost," said Pamela.

Fedora regarded her uneasily. "I don't understand."

"You don't have any damned business following us around."

Fedora looked at me.

"I don't tell her what to say," I said.

His eyes narrowed. "Okay, you two. You're adults. You call yourselves detectives." He looked at Pamela.

I thought she might give him the finger. She didn't, but her left eyebrow went up. The eyebrow told him to screw himself.

"Just what kind of case is it you're on now?" he asked her.

"Are you going to be civilized or do John and I have to start calling for lawyers and stuff like that?"

He looked at me.

"She's got a point," I said.

"Okay, okay," said Fedora.

"I'm looking for an *objet d'art*," said Pamela.

Fedora looked at me.

"The same," I said.

Fedora rested his forehead on the heel of his hand. "Sure, sure," he said sarcastically. "Just how does a girl named Leanne Armstrong fit into this?"

"Well, there are these twin sisters in my home town. One,

115

name of Linda, wants to know where the other is. The other's name is Leanne, as you know. She's here in Seattle somewhere. I said I'd see what I could do. As a favor."

"As a favor?" said Fedora.

"That's right." I wondered how Steve McQueen would play that scene.

"What does that have to do with a piece of art?"

"I don't know. You'd have to ask Ms. Yew here about that."

Fedora looked disgusted. "You expect me to believe that?"

"Mr. Denson doesn't know what he's looking for," said Pamela.

"Well, then, you tell me the connection," he said to Pamela.

"No," she said.

"No."

"No. If I tell you that, John Denson here will know what he's after." That struck her as funny and she began laughing.

"Listen," I said. "What was the name of your agency again?"

Fedora stared at me patiently. "You're in the big leagues, Denson. Be a knothead and you're gonna be sorry. You too, Ms. Yew. I'm telling you both this for your own good."

"You're telling us who's in the big leagues! You can't stay covert on a guy who takes a walk for a head of cauliflower and a glass of beer."

There was no doubt now that Fedora was grinding his jaw muscles. He probably wanted to sock me in the mouth but he restrained himself. "You want we should have the local fuzz haul the two of you in and put you on ice for a few days?"

"On what charge?"

"There's lots of charges laying around. The locals are smart enough. They'll come up with something."

"Are you after the girl?"

Fedora looked at me.

"I said, are you after the girl?"

"She's part of it," he said.

"But not the whole part."

He didn't say anything.

It seemed like everybody knew what was going on except me. "I want the girl safe," I said.

"So do we."

"Then why don't you help me out instead of following me around town all day and pushing me around in here. That doesn't make any sense. Does that make any sense, Pamela?"

"None at all," she said. Well delivered: flip and irreverent.

"Believe it or not, we don't want you two to wind up with your heads mashed in. You're playing with a fast crowd."

"I think we've been through this before," I said. I massaged the stubble on my chin.

"Will you back off or do you wait it out downtown?"

"Will you let us know what's going on?"

"No."

"No?" asked Pamela.

"No."

Fedora thought he had us on the run. Overcoat was in high spirits. Fedora looked at me over his beer glass. "If you'd let us know what you've found out maybe we can get this over a little quicker."

"Pamela said no. I go along with that."

"They don't know anything anyway," said Shoulders.

"I'd make book," said Overcoat.

Fedora thought about it.

"Lay off us and we'll think about scratching backs," I said.

"Speak for yourself," said Pamela.

"What?"

"I said speak for yourself."

"Are you two working together?" Overcoat gave me a derisive snicker.

I shrugged. "Won't be too hard to find out who you are. With guys like you, it can't be a very classy agency."

Fedora laughed at Overcoat. Poor Overcoat.

"I suppose Shoulders here will write the report this time out," I said, looking at Fedora. "You don't want the job and I can't imagine Overcoat here remembering verbs and stuff like that."

Overcoat twisted on the wooden bench and glared at me.

"Oh, calm down Alb . . ." began Shoulders. He stopped and looked quickly at Fedora.

117

"No harm done," said Fedora. "Shall we be going gentlemen?" He stood up. Shoulders and Overcoat followed. They all three filed out the door and left Pamela Yew and me sitting there with a half-empty pitcher of beer.

"Who were those guys?" asked the bartender when he gathered up the dirty glasses.

"Could be anybody from the FBI to the Treasury Department," I said.

"Huh?" The bartender laughed an oh-sure laugh.

"Maybe even the Central Intelligence Agency, though that's hardly likely."

"Who do you think?" asked Pamela.

"I don't know. I thought maybe you could tell me."

Pamela Yew was concerned. "I tell you honestly, John, that I don't have any idea of why the government would be interested in this. This is as big a mystery to me as it is to you."

"You do know who the guy in the fedora was?"

She nodded yes. "He was the same guy who nearly ran over us minutes after Sally Whipple had her throat cut at that awful strip joint."

"The same," I said.

Eleven

PAMELA YEW AND I went our separate ways after our fun with Sam's boys. I wondered why the federal government would be interested in a piece of art. But Pamela, at least, knew what she was looking for. I didn't. I found a diner, bought a newspaper and a cup of coffee, and settled down to relax. I didn't relax long.

On the first page of the metro section was a photograph of a young woman who had been left naked in a filthy alley, beaten to within an inch of her life. Both eyes were swollen shut. She had lost several teeth, not to mention her bruises and two fractured ribs.

Her assailant had left her in the cold rain with a tag wired around her neck. The tag was to the point: "Listen up, sister. Be back by sundown or I'll finish what I started."

The story was by Wayne Phillips. It said the woman, in shock and unable to talk, was under police guard at the hospital. The police did not know her name. They didn't know who her sister was, either.

I knew her name. I also knew her sister. She was Linda Armstrong Hammond. A sadist she had married, for reasons known only to her, had grown tired of waiting for me to call.

Why spend a dime for a telephone call when you can get the newspapers to run your message for free? All you have to do is mash your wife's face in and the photographers will compete to record the results. All of Seattle got to participate in the fun over a cup of coffee.

I was enraged—enraged at her pain, at her humiliation, at the invasion of her privacy. I was enraged at Hammond's assumption that he was out of harm's way, that nobody, not the police, not me, could do anything to stop him from having his way. I amused him; I didn't even carry a gun.

Well, I was smarter than him. What I could do was take from him whatever it was Pamela Yew was after and see his rear in prison. Nobody was gonna stop me.

I looked at the picture again and felt sick, impotent, because I had tried to be civilized.

I thought about calling Wayne Phillips to go with me to the hospital but decided against it. I might find something useful; I needed more for a quid pro quo. When I got to the hospital I found Sergeant Timothy Drummond in charge. Timmy was an okay guy. He was one of the best volleyball players in the department. He played the guitar and wasn't a bad painter. He also had a daughter Linda's age.

I told Timmy the girl's name and asked if I could go inside. Timmy tugged at his belt and looked up and down the hall.

"You say her name's Linda Armstrong Hammond," he said. He made a note on a small pad.

"Like I say, she used to be a neighbor of mine back home."

Timmy bit his lip. "I'm under orders not to let anybody in there, Denson. The doctors don't want anybody to talk to her. She's still in shock or something."

"The last thing in the world I want to do is upset her. Be a guy, Timmy; I gave you her name."

Timmy sighed. "You didn't used to carry a piece. How about now?"

"Still clear," I said. I raised my arms if he wanted to frisk me.

"Three minutes, no more," said Timmy. "I'll be watching."

When I saw Linda Hammond's face, I knew Phillips hadn't hyped his story. Both of her eyes were nearly swollen shut. I couldn't tell if she was asleep or awake. I moved to the side of the bed and looked into the puffy black pits. I thought I saw movement there and I was right: she blinked one painful blink. I didn't know if she recognized me or not. I turned to Timmy; he was staring at the floor. He wanted to get the guy who had done this to her; he thought I might be of help.

Linda made an indeterminate noise with her swollen mouth. It looked like her teeth had almost gone through her lips in spots.

"You take it easy now and let me put my ear down there," I said.

The black pits blinked.

I leaned over.

She made another sound. I shook my head. I couldn't understand her. She tried again with my ear almost touching her lips.

"Looked wrong," she breathed.

"I don't understand."

"Ducks on it. Didn't look right. Decoys."

"Ducks on what, Linda?"

The swollen lips moved again. "Flowers."

"Flowers?"

"China."

Timmy leaned through the open door. "Better hurry it up, John."

"What else, Linda?" I whispered.

"Hashita Maru." She was very clear. That would be a Japanese vessel of some kind. A merchant vessel, possibly. That must be it.

She tried to speak again but her whisper was stopped by pain. She started trembling.

I stood up. The *Hashita Maru* was the break I needed. I also had a clue of sorts to Pamela Yew's mystery object. Decoys. Ducks. Flowers. China.

The black pits blinked. They were asking me a question.

I leaned over and whispered into her ear: "I'll figure it out, Linda, everything will be okay."

"Leanne," she breathed.

"I know."

"What did she say, John?" asked Timmy.

"She asked me to look after her sister and I said I would." I stepped out into the hall.

Timmy closed the door. "I'd like to get my hands on the bastard who did that to her."

"So would I."

"Do you have any ideas?"

"Not really," I said. "If I get any, I'll let you people know first thing." I started off down the hall.

"Wait a minute, you'll have to go downtown and tell them . . ."

I didn't want to hear the rest of what he had to say. I didn't have time for long-winded discussions with the Seattle police. I slipped through a door and was gone.

Once I got outside the hospital I looked up and down the street for a pay telephone. There was one in the lobby but I knew there would be cops coming in and out. Once Timmy Drummond told them I knew the girl's name they would be asking questions. There was a pay phone at the corner of a gas station parking lot a couple of blocks from the hospital. I called Wayne Phillips at the *Star*.

"Wayne, Denson here."

"Hey, man, how's it going? Been gettin' the stuff on our little story?"

"Is our deal still on with regard to those heavies and the twins?"

"If you've got something worthwhile to swap, I guess so."

"Can you talk? I mean, Charley Powell's not hanging over your shoulder or anything like that?"

"I'm by myself. What'cha got?"

I decided to gamble. If I was wrong I wouldn't be much use to Wayne Phillips. But it was now or maybe never.

"Do the Feds know the ship it's coming in on?" I asked. I held my breath. It seemed to take Phillips forever to answer.

"No, they don't," he said.

I cleared my throat. "How about you?"

"How about me what?"

"Do you know what ship it's coming in on?"

Phillips laughed a wheezing laugh. "If the Feds don't know how would I know?"

"Then you're getting your dope from the Feds?"

Phillips didn't say anything. He'd been bad. He didn't want me to know his source.

"How in the hell did you manage that?" I asked.

"Just what is it you have to swap, Denson?"

"The name of the ship. Just what is it you know, Phillips, anything?"

"Well, there's a ship due in Vancouver."

"That's a starter. How do you know that?"

"Chickie told me."

"What chickie? What are you talking about?"

"Can't make any difference to you."

"A girl?"

"That's it, Mac."

"What girl? It's possible we got it from the same place." Phillips could have been there when the police questioned Linda.

"I got promises to keep, bub, you know this business."

"A secretary?"

Phillips didn't answer.

It was a secretary. "Good work," I said.

"What's the ship?"

"Swap you for the cargo."

"Done."

"The *Hashita Maru.*"

"Heroin. Maybe a couple of million bucks worth. The Feds don't know for sure."

Heroin. My God! Had Pamela Yew lied to me about thing mineral on top of everything else? It's not hard to shade the truth with two million bucks on the line. But what about ducks-decoys-flowers-China? What was that? "Does your gal know how a punk like Hammond managed to play in that kind of league?"

"Listen, every time one of those Feds breaks wind he's gotta write a report; you know that. My gal has to type the damned things. You got it doped out now. I don't have to tell you that word of this gets out, she loses her job; I lose a friend and a helluva source. You get the picture?"

For Phillips that was real emotion.

"I get the picture. How about the rest of it?"

"Your friend Hammond flew pot out of the Golden Triangle, didn't he? He knows how to take care of himself. He's good; on that everyone agrees. The word got out and the CIA got in touch, kind of like the Yankees spotting a hot kid from Boise. The agency used him for jobs that were too hairy for their own people. You do that kind of work, you pick up contacts. That's been eight years or more ago but a guy like Hammond keeps in touch. He's still in the business; the government knows that."

"Smuggling?"

"Yes, smuggling."

"Just dope."

"Anything he can get his hands on."

Ah, comes the quest of Pamela Yew. Ducks-decoys-flowers-China was something being smuggled in from Asia. But what? "Are you certain they know all that?"

"Listen, this little gal ain't making this all up. She may be a secretary but she isn't stupid."

"Well, you might as well give me the rest of it," I said.

"I'm telling you everything I know. How do I know I'm not going to get screwed in this deal?"

"Come on, man. I'll see you get a helluva story."

Phillips sighed. "In this current deal, one of Hammond's old contacts apparently arranged for him to meet a Chinese in Hong Kong, who would see to it that transportation was arranged."

"The Hong Kong gentleman no doubt has friends in the Seattle Chinese community."

"You've got ESP, bub."

"The Chinese at this end think they'll zap Hammond once he gets the stuff into the U.S., but he thinks he's smarter than they are."

"Something like that," said Phillips.

"But the Chinese have gone to cover."

124

"Very."

I could see it unfolding. "Let me see if I can guess the rest. Hammond, by agreement with the Chinese, made some smaller test runs last summer. The tests went smoothly. Hammond decided to eliminate his help in case they got ideas about cutting themselves in on too large a share. That would be Tony Whipple and Jimmy Petrick. But his new crew, Lewis Cooper and Larry Fowler, somehow found out about the size of the final run. They went to cover and took Leanne Armstrong with them."

Phillips whistled. "You're clairvoyant, Sherlock."

"She went with them because she was hooked on samples lifted from the smaller runs."

"That makes sense," said Phillips.

"That's when Hammond decided to engage the services of a private detective to help him out?"

"What?"

"I guess I didn't tell you that. It was Hammond who put me on Leanne's trail."

"Oh, boy," said Phillips.

"One mean sucker."

"What do we do now?" Phillips asked.

I had to be way ahead of Pamela, except for not knowing the exact nature of ducks-decoys-flowers-China. "I think we should let the federal people know about the *Hashita Maru,* but deal ourselves in on the noose."

"Think they'll go along with that?"

"Who have you been getting your information from?"

"Now I'd hate like hell to tell you that, Denson. There are lots of secretaries in a town like this, and what with reports and memoranda floating around . . ."

"Who's the one whose name begins with Alb?"

Phillips paused. "That would be George Alben. New man here."

"How about the one who wears a snappy green fedora?"

"Clint Johns."

"Guy with big shoulders."

"Tony Butterfield. Know any more?"

125

"No."

"There are more in town, a visiting battalion. Those three are assigned here."

"I'll see what I can work out," I said. "I'll keep in touch."

"Solid."

"One more thing. Did you wangle a check on that license number I gave you on the Porsche?"

He had. He gave me a North Side address. Up near the zoo.

"Thanks much," I said. I hung up and called the Longshore-man's Union for more details on the *Hashita Maru,* then drove back to my apartment. I relaxed with a bottle of Mackeson's, and at eleven p.m. turned on the tube and watched an old movie. It was William Powell, Myrna Loy, Ruth Hussey, and Otto Kruger in a Thin Man movie. The blurb in the Sunday television magazine said it featured Irish wolfhounds, burned bath houses, and escaped convicts. How can you lose with that?

After the movie I set the alarm, crawled into bed, and listened to the traffic outside for half an hour. Then I let the fantasies come. Over the years I'd had several favorites which I'd eventually tired of, like a record or a certain kind of food. None of the fantasies had an ending. If there had been an ending, it would have destroyed the promise of the beginning and that was the whole point. They were invariably romantic and melodramatic. Some were better than others. I usually went to those immediately. I often went to the middle and when no ending was in sight, retreated to the beginning. Beginnings were nice. As to the endings, I knew I'd never make it that far. But I tried anyway.

This time Pamela Yew's face kept interfering. So I tried to resurrect a fantasy from my youth. There was one that had once had a long run, for months had shown no signs of petering out. I recalled it for the hell of it as one sometimes remembers a lost love, wondering what was the attraction. In the fantasy I was a bright young guy who had lifted himself up from a modest if not poor background by sheer talent. The chief honcho of a large corporation took a liking to me because I was personable, bright, and presumably something like the son he never had. I never was sure exactly what the corporation

126

did or made. I spent a lot of time drinking Wild Turkey whiskey with the old boy in his den where we swore a lot, told jokes, and shot pool. We talked about hunting geese, fishing, and football. He liked my storytelling and responded to the punch lines with loud and booming if not vulgar laughter.

It was the old man's laughter that disturbed his daughter. She was a gorgeous thing, a graduate of Vassar or some place like that, and spent her time skiing in the Alps or drinking Mai Tais in Acapulco. It was obvious that her father considered her boyfriends borderline homosexuals but he didn't say anything. Well, whenever her friends were in the house and her father broke into one of his Ernest Hemingway fits of laughter at one of my wisecracks, she would appear in the den and tell him to please hold it down. She looked through me like I was a bug or something or didn't exist. Sometimes when she did this she would drag one of her boyfriends along with her. The boyfriends always looked with distaste at the stuffed fish and old books on the walls. In those situations I just stood there like a dumb-ass and chalked my cue or stared at my feet, feeling like an unwanted interloper, aware that my jacket was out of style and rumpled.

Anyway, the daughter had an enormous bash in the house one night. She and her friends were drinking and carrying on throughout the house while her father and I held forth in the den, drinking whiskey and shooting pool. Sometime during the night there was an enormous row in the living room; the father and I emerged from the den just in time to see this sucker slap the daughter in the face and shove her around. I strolled through the gathering of lovely people like Clint Eastwood and casually kneed the guy in the stomach as hard as I could. He fell over and began vomiting on the white shag carpet. The father and I returned to our game.

So the daughter wound up drunk with a torn dress in the driving rain on the streets at four a.m. I picked her up and took her to my apartment because she said she didn't want to go home. The memory is dim here, it was so long ago. I do know I picked her up. She passed out on the way. I had to drag her inside, take her wet clothes off, dry her with a towel, and stuff her in my bed. In the fantasy I had clean sheets for once. I slept on the couch like Cary Grant or somebody. The next morning, while I was taking a shower, she got dressed and slipped out the front door.

A couple of nights later, as the old man was racking up the balls, he said his daughter wanted to know my name. Later on, she showed up to watch the game and listen to our carrying on. She even got the whiskey out of the cabinet.

So there it was: honor rewarded. A giver acknowledged and loved.

It was there that the fantasy got fuzzy. There was an obvious potential for a romantic ending, but even as a young man I could never bring it off to the end. The prize had to be there but I was afraid of what it might turn out to be.

It was raining. I sat up, turned on the light by my bed, and thought about the fantasy. I remembered it all clearly. I listened to the rain. Pamela Yew was in Seattle that night, possibly listening to the rain as well. What were her fantasies as a young woman? I got myself a drink of water and settled back in bed, but I was still haunted by the memory of that past dream.

Twelve

I WAS JUST ABOUT TO drift off to sleep when the telephone rang. It was Jerry Hammond.

"Denson, old fucker," he began. He was trying to sound like a long-lost buddy.

"That's me."

"You're off the case, boy. If I catch you asking any more questions about my sister-in-law, I'll cut your heart out, understand."

"But I'm not finished."

"I'm afraid you are, old pal. I'm not much of a sport, you know that. I'm afraid you're not worth a pinch as a detective anyhow. I found Leanne on my own. Just sent word out and in she came. They always come running sooner or later, broads like that." Hammond laughed on the other end of the line.

"Listen, dammit," I said.

"Listen dammit what? You keep it up and here's what will happen, friend. Just before I work you over, I'll maybe find your girlfriend with the long hair and do a little carving with my trusty old toadstabber. Understand now? Her mother's initials maybe. Something sentimental."

Pamela Yew. "I understand." What's more, I believed him.

129

Jerry Hammond hung up.

I phoned his number in Cayuse. A telephone operator answered:

"I'm sorrreee, the number you called has been disconnected."

I hung up. The telephone rang again.

It was Hammond.

"What is it this time?" I asked.

"I've had second thoughts, Denson. I'm not at all a bad guy. You have to understand that. I'm ready to deal if I can get something out of it. You talk to some Feds the last couple days?"

"Just this afternoon." How did he know? Was he following me? No. He had to be guessing.

"You gonna keep in touch?"

"Well, I don't know. I guess I could. What do you have in mind?" Jerry Hammond had use for me.

"You keeping up on what the Feds're doing in exchange for Leanne's hide, and me laying off your long-haired girlfriend."

I figured I may as well work a deal and wonder how I was being used later. "And Linda," I said. "All three of them."

"Okay then, all three." He was agreeing too quickly.

"When do we make the swap?"

"We meet first, talk it over."

"When?"

Hammond clicked his tongue. "Tonight, at a joint out in the country where I can be sure you're not being tailed."

"Name it." Big Man. I was nuts.

"It's called Big Bill's Bar. You take Interstate 90 East to the Hunt's Road Exit, that's a few miles past Issaquah. You take Hunt's Road south—there'll be a Texaco station and an all-night cafe there, a truck stop—and drive about six miles until you come to Beaver Flats. Ain't much of a place. Gas station and Big Bill's. That's it. Now Bill's has a front porch; the porch has a night light. Be under that light any time from closing till the sun comes up. Place closes at three a.m. Leave your car up the road a piece, say one hundred yards. You should be able to walk that far, healthy guy like you."

"I'll be there."

"Alone."

"I don't need help with a jerk like you."

Hammond hung up again.

Hunt's Road was about twenty miles east of Seattle. There was a Texaco gas station and an all-night truck stop restaurant at the off-ramp. I swung off the Interstate and headed south on Hunt's Road, as Hammond had directed. Mt. Rainier rose up directly in front of me, soft white under the moon. The moon had a circle around it. It was a cold night; I kept the heater going in my Fiat. The glow over Seattle was behind me and to my right.

Hunt's Road took one lazy swing to the left, then passed through some farmhouses. The farmhouses went quickly and there was nothing, just me, the barbed wire on either side of the road, and Mt. Rainier. For a while the car radio was picking up a bizarre rock station from out of the Southern California ionosphere. Then the music faded, crowded out by a Seattle station. I turned it off.

Hammond was right about the distance to Beaver Flats. It was almost six miles on the nose. I could see the trees in the moonlight. When I entered the trees I could see there was nothing to Beaver Flats except for an old Mobil gas station with old-fashioned round pumps, and Big Bill's Bar. I didn't care about the Mobil station. Big Bill's was on my mind. I parked my car down the road like I was told and walked on to Bill's. There was an old plank porch out front with a red Coca-Cola machine and a bench where you could sit. I sat. The neon sign on the painted-glass window said Bill served Olympia on tap. I waited. No Hammond. I figured he was out there under the trees somewhere watching for cops. My feet were cold. I could have used a barking dog. Where were they when you needed them? I waited in silence.

When Hammond appeared, he came like a shadow under the single yellow lightbulb above Big Bill's porch. I didn't hear anything. I just turned and there he was, standing by the Coke machine with a big grin on his face.

"Denson?" he said amiably.

"Me," I said and got up off the cold bench. On a sunny day

131

it was probably a good bench for old men. Nice place to whittle and remember. I was beginning to get the idea I might never qualify for my social security.

Hammond pulled a switchblade from out of his tight-fitting Levi's. The bottoms of the Levi's were tucked into the tops of cowboy boots with turquoise leather, silver toes and great big heels. Funny he had that knife in his hands and I stared at his boots.

"Hell of a pair of boots you've got there."

"Cost me seventy-five bucks. Fucked the others up on your mouth. Scarred 'em."

"Should have let me know," I said.

"Man can't have teeth marks on his boots. What'd people think?"

"I can understand that."

"Yes sir, pissed me off." Hammond flipped the toadstabber once and looked at it carefully in the dim light. Then he pressed something and a blade appeared without a sound. The blade was like a snake's tongue; only it stayed there.

I started unzipping my pants. "Give me a second to take a piss, Hammond, and I'll take that thing away from you and shove it up your ass." I flat turned my back on Hammond and his knife. I took four lazy steps toward the corner of Big Bill's Bar, then took off like a gut-shot deer.

Let me tell you I ran. My wonderful apparatus was shifting in the breeze but I didn't have time for such civilized details as putting the thing back in place.

I heard Hammond mutter "Jesus Christ!", then there was nothing but the thud, thud, thud of his cowboy boots.

It was him and me.

He was bigger, stronger, faster, and meaner than I was but he was wearing cowboy boots. I had on my Nike go-fasts, left over from the days when I thought I wanted to jog to blow the fat out of my veins. The only thing I could think of was that blade and the advice my high school track coach gave me to breathe through my nose as long as possible to warm up the air on the way to my lungs. That had been twenty years ago

132

but I still remembered. You can shred your lungs on a cold day, he said.

I breathed through my nose and concentrated on the road ahead. I figured maybe a half mile and I could give him the slip.

The boots kept coming.

I kept moving.

I made the half-mile okay, but I forgot one detail. There was a tightly stretched five-strand barbed wire fence on each side of the road, designed to keep the cows off Hunt's Road. If I tried to climb that fence Hammond would leave a gaping hole up my spine. The only thing I could do was keep moving.

I kept moving. Rainier was at my back now; the glow over Seattle was up front. It was six miles to the all-night restaurant, if I could hold out.

I opened up about a forty-yard lead on Hammond, then paced myself. If the thud, thuds came faster, I moved faster. When the thud, thuds slowed, I slowed.

It was about twenty minutes before Hammond said anything.

"I'm gonna cut your nuts off, Denson."

I didn't say anything.

"Hear me?"

I kept my mouth shut. My thighs were burning up. My arms were so tired I couldn't keep them high where they could help me breathe. My shins ached. My lungs burned. I kept going. If I thought about the pain it would get worse. I had to think of something else.

I thought about a drunk I met one night in a bar in Portland. He said he had once been a professor of anthropology at the University of Oregon but lost his job when a coed accused him of screwing her in exchange for a grade. It wasn't true, he said, but then there was a big fuss in the papers. He said the university administrators said they were sorry but the school got its money from the state legislature. He said the truth was he hadn't done anything with the student.

"Should have least gotten the satisfaction," said the bartender.

"Should've," the professor agreed.

One thing led to another and he began talking about the

133

aborigines of Australia. He wanted to know if we knew how an aborigine with a club kills a kangaroo in the desert. Keep in mind there isn't any good cover for an ambush, he said. Just the aborigine and the kangaroo. One on one. The professor paused there and didn't say anything. Just sipped his drink.

"Go on," I said. It was a curious problem.

"Well, you see, a kangaroo is a hopping animal. Man is a running animal."

"So?"

"So an aborigine knows the difference. He waits on a trail or maybe at a waterhole somewhere until he spots his kangaroo. He starts out after the kangaroo at a trot. The kangaroo bounds away. The aborigine keeps coming. The kangaroo bounds away again. And so on. That night the aborigine gets some sleep; he knows the kangaroo is curious. It'll be around the next morning. When the aborigine spots it, he starts trotting again. Repeats the whole business."

"Well, how does he get the kangaroo?" the bartender asked.

"After about three or four days the kangaroo wakes up on a cold morning with charley horses in his legs, terrible cramps. It can't move. The aborigine rushes it and thumps it on the head. Difference of muscles. Aborigine knows that."

The professor peered at me over his highball glass.

"Aborigine just waits him out," I said.

"That's it," said the professor.

"So what does that have to do with anything?" asked the bartender.

"Some of us are hoppers, some are runners." The professor grinned. He thought it was a hell of a story.

"Is that true about the kangaroos?" I asked.

"I don't know," he said. "I doubt it."

I had the feeling, listening to Hammond's boots thumping behind me, that it was true. It was true and I was a hopper. Jim Sullivan was a runner. Pamela Yew was a hopper turned runner. Hammond was a runner. I was a hopper. But I was a smart hopper. That was the difference. I kept my feet moving. I kept my feet moving and watched the sparkle of the moonlight off broken beer bottles on the road shoulders and on the

134

ditch between the shoulders and the barbed wire. Even the barbed wire glistened. There was the moon, the broken glass, the wire and the glow over Seattle. And Hammond. I don't know how long it took us to cover the six miles. All I know was that the red sun was coming over Rainier by the time I saw the sign high above the Texaco station.

I was still running.

Hammond was only about thirty yards behind me. We slowed to a walk. I could hear his ragged breathing behind me. I was alive still and even had my penis back in my pants like a gentleman.

When we got within about one hundred yards of the truck-stop, Hammond spoke again. It was the first thing he had said since near the beginning.

"Denson?"

"Yes." I decided I could spare the energy now that safety was in sight. I didn't turn my head. I listened to his boots.

Boots and breathing, nothing more.

"You're a dead man, Denson."

"You told me that already," I said.

"Remember it."

"How can I forget?"

Thank God the truck stop was full of drivers having break-fast. I slipped onto a stool at the counter and ordered a cup of coffee and watched as Hammond followed me inside. The waitress gave me a strange look when I gave her a buck for the coffee. My hands trembled and she could see my shirt was drenched with sweat. I had to hold onto the counter to keep from falling down.

"Been a hard night," I said.

"Looks it," the waitress said.

I took fifteen cents from the change and called Pamela Yew.

"Huh?" she said.

I told her what had happened.

"You damned fool."

"Are you calling me a damned fool?"

"You're a fool, Mr. Denson. I'll be there in half an hour."

When I hung up I saw that Hammond had settled himself on

135

the stool next to mine. He grinned at me with his white sparklers.

"Who'd you call?"

"Cops," I said.

"Needn't have bothered." He nodded toward a Washington State highway patrolman I hadn't seen. The patrolman was having some breakfast at the far end of the counter.

"Join me?" asked Hammond.

"Why not," I said and reclaimed my stool. Neither of us could pick up a cup of coffee without our hands trembling.

"Why look at your hands, a-shaking like that," he said.

We each ordered breakfast and ate without another word. When he finished, Hammond got up and paid his bill. Mine too.

"This one's on me, Denson."

I didn't say anything.

Then he leaned over and whispered in my ear. "I've got a big ol' .357 magnum at home. Has an eight-inch barrel. Pretty sucker. And you know what? The next time I see you, I'm gonna take that sucker and blow your head off." He grinned at me again. "Got myself some hollow points. Used one to drop a big old mule deer up to Meacham last year. Four point. There wasn't anything left except horns and hooves. Damned shame. Ruin all that meat."

"Wasted your tag," I said.

"I don't waste tags. I let him go and got me another one. Broke his neck clean with that .357. All John Law knew I used a little old Model 94 Winchester I carried around with me. Pea shooter."

"I don't do much hunting."

"Just think of what that .357 would do to a man."

I did. After Hammond left I went into the john and vomited from exhaustion.

Pamela didn't say anything for the first mile or so while we rode back to Big Bill's and my Fiat. She looked at me slumped on the passenger's side in exhaustion.

"So what did you try to do, John Denson?"

I watched as she geared down for a stoplight. "I thought I could talk to him."

"Oh, yeah, what makes you think you could do that?"

"I don't know." My hands were still shaking. The distance seemed a lot shorter this morning. I watched the barbed wire.

"What did he tell you?"

"He put you on his list."

"Ahh," she said. "He called me as well. You do know I carry a piece, John Denson?"

"Oh, yes, I know that."

"That's more than you."

"Yes."

"I know how to use it."

"I expect so."

"Then why did you go out there?"

"There's part of me that said I had to do it. If it didn't work out it would have been right and proper."

Pamela Yew grinned. "Honorable? Manly?"

"Something like that."

"How many times have I saved your skull since we've been at this business?"

I looked at her. "Twice, I guess."

"Why d'you suppose I gave a damn?"

I closed my eyes and opened them again.

"I kicked Hammond in the crotch for the same reason you met him out there in the middle of the night. Only I don't have Lancelot, the Virginian and Philip Marlowe as heroes. Do me a favor, will you?"

"What's that?"

"Do me the favor of letting me take my knocks if I'm gonna play your game."

I smiled. "What the hell, Ms. Yew."

"Huh?"

"It's we men who lay down our cloaks and our lives."

Pamela Yew shook her head. "While we women stay on our pedestal, eh?"

I knew what she was saying. "That's it, I guess."

"Well, I want down, John Denson. If you win your bet you'll find I'm made of flesh and blood. No big deal."

She was probably right about that. "But didn't you like it that I laid it on the line?"

"Yes, I liked it. And no, I didn't. I was flattered and I was pissed."

We were just down the road from Big Bill's Bar. John Denson, knight errant, got out of Pamela Yew's BMW and wobbled over to his Fiat. I looked back at her. "It's not easy to play your game, Ms. Yew. Old habits are hard to break."

"Try." She grinned.

"I'll do my best." I would, too. But it's true what I told her, old habits are not easy to break.

Thirteen

THE NEXT DAY I DECIDED to follow up on the yellow Porsche. It was now my only link to Leanne, to Hammond and to whatever it was that was ducks-decoys-flowers-China. The address Phillips had given me from the registration papers in Olympia was in a wealthy area of east Seattle. It was a split-level brick house with trees and a lovely lawn, the stuff of the American dream. I assumed it was Hammond's. I had to smile at that. I once read where only 7 percent of the American population was the classic family—the mother, father, and two children. Father off to work. Mother home waxing floors.

The rest of us, the Pamela Yews and the John Densons, comprised a 93 percent statistical eberration, failures by definition.

Nor did it surprise me that Jerry Hammond should own a house like that. Did it matter that he was a smuggler and a murderer? Was that relevant? He no doubt made more money than a member of the healing professions. I had to be careful in casing the place. If I rang the door and Hammond answered, he likely as not would kick me in the stomach. Or maybe gouge an eye out. That's a CIO's idea of fun. If Leanne saw me walking up the sidewalk she would likely as not bolt and leave me with close to nothing to go on.

I bought some raw broccoli, a bag of Cheetos, and a six-pack of Bass ale from a corner grocery store and holed up in my Fiat. That left me with a long wait and a whole lot of time to think.

Why was I staying with the case? Was it because of Leanne Armstrong? Not really, although she was part of it. Pamela Yew? Yes. Pamela Yew kept her distance so it was hard to know whether she was attracted to me or not. Yet I had made the bet. Why had I done that? Was it because she was free? Did I want to somehow possess her and rob her of that just to prove I could do it? No. I wanted her to succeed on her terms and I wanted to win my bet. I wanted both.

She survived by being careful. She was careful of me. Yet I wondered if she were not somehow a romantic as I was, a dreamer who kept her dreams to herself for fear they and she would be smashed. She had her men. No woman of her presence and intellect is without men. Men cling to women like Pamela Yew like determined cockleburs. I had never met her men. I was envious of them. I wondered if they were not the great irony of her life, her decoys.

I massaged my thighs. My legs were beginning to knot from my moonlight run. What if my legs cramped and Hammond found me? I kept moving them so as not to be a literal hopper. No doubt Hammond was holed up somewhere having his legs pummeled by a gorgeous masseuse who gave real massages, then threw in a little extra.

The rain started again. My breath fogged up the interior of the Fiat. No matter; I didn't want anybody to see me anyway.

A brown Chevrolet eased down the street. That was the second time it had passed in the last three hours. Pamela Yew? I didn't think so. She was probably on the same street I was, sitting, like me, behind fogged-up windows. Maybe Sam's boys from downtown. I hunkered down on the seat in hopes of not being seen. It wasn't so bad in the Fiat. My raincoat kept me relatively warm but my feet were cold. Like waiting for geese.

By eleven p.m., I had finished my Cheetos, my broccoli, and my last bottle of ale. Still no Porsche.

I looked up and down the street wondering which car held

Pamela Yew. A few days earlier I wouldn't have believed she had the stuff to wait it out by herself in a stakeout. I knew better now. Working alone wasn't the best proposition. You couldn't sleep. You got no relief. You had to pay attention.

Sometime around one a.m., I fell asleep. A couple of hours later I sat up with a start and whacked my knee against the steering column in the process. I assumed the cold had jarred me awake. I wiped another hole in the moisture and lo, there was the yellow Porsche parked in front of the big house. There were lights on in the house so the car must have just arrived. It, and not the cold, was why I woke up.

I watched the Porsche. Nothing.

The lights went out across the way. Leanne would get some sleep. She would be there in the morning.

It would be possible to get back to my apartment, shower, shave, and get a couple of hours of sleep before returning to my post at six. Sunrise over Seattle and all that. I eased the Fiat out of the neighborhood and was on my way home when a car pulled up on my tail and blinked its lights.

I pulled over. Pamela Yew pulled alongside and rolled down the window.

"Gonna take a little nap, Mr. Denson?" She giggled.

I got almost two hours of sleep before I was back on the line. My mouth tasted sour but I was relatively sober. After an hour of waiting, my stomach began to gurgle; I had a slight case of the shakes. But I was determined to stick it out. No woman was going to beat me.

At ten o'clock the front door of the house opened; Leanne Armstrong stepped out and strode briskly to the Porsche. She drove a few blocks, turned left, and headed toward downtown. She had missed rush hour; there was little traffic. Unfortunately, the street she chose had lots of stop lights. Worse yet, Leanne was a driver who timed her lights so she could glide through the greens. I had to hang back; that left me with ambers and an occasional red. That was better than Pamela Yew, who was tailing me in her Ford. She ran nine red lights, cold. I counted them all before a Seattle cop pulled her over. I flashed my hazard lights to let her know I had seen her in my rearview mirror.

I bet the civilized Ms. Yew had bad words to say. Love that cop.

Leanne drove straight to a large department store. She parked her Porsche in a private lot and so did I. Then it was on to the third floor, via escalator. The third floor was mostly ladies' clothing—casual wear, evening wear and lingerie. Leanne was wearing an expensive, new-looking blue coat. I eased over to the coat section, found a chair, and pretended I was waiting for a wife or girlfriend. I had thought about setting up in a corner of the floor that featured specials but I thought better of it. Good thinking. The first thing Leanne did was head for the bargain section where she stood, fingering various items for twenty-five minutes. I was hungry as hell and wondered how long she would prolong her ritual. From the bargain area she went to the lingerie section where she again stood in front of racks fingering various items.

Leanne finally bought something. Panties, it looked like, possibly a slip. From there she went to a dress section. Although it was still January, the store was displaying its spring line. It must have been fun; she spent fifty minutes trying on pastel dresses. The clerk enthused over each selection but Leanne was not easily satisfied. At last she made a selection, a green dress made of silky-appearing material.

She headed for the elevator. It was lunch time; Leanne stopped at a coffee shop and had a cheeseburger and a glass of milk. I watched, listening to my stomach grumble. My only consolation was that Pamela Yew had been sidetracked by the Seattle police. I was one up on her in the race for the decoy-flowers-China. Whatever that was. Mineral. Was Pamela not thinking or had she meant that literally? A painting canvas is made of cotton. The base for paint is oil—at least traditionally. That was mineral. But what about the pigments themselves? I assumed some of the color came from vegetables, some from animals, and still others from minerals. She was most likely after a painting. Pamela was either lying to sidetrack me or hadn't thought when she gave me my answer. If somebody

142

asked me if an oil painting was animal, mineral, or vegetable, I'd answer mineral without thinking.

After her cheeseburger, Leanne got into her Porsche, turned left and headed west. My Fiat got trapped in the parking lot by a white-haired lady trying to park a Chrysler. I lost my rabbit. Once I shed the old lady, I zipped up the street and in four blocks caught my quarry again, a bit of luck I could hardly believe.

Leanne took the Porsche up the ramp for Interstate 5 North and hit the accelerator. She topped out at seventy-five, which pushed my 1300 cc Fiat. I could go faster but didn't like to. The pair of us headed toward Bellingham, Canada, Alaska, and points north.

Someone had given her sound instructions on a routine and simple way of clearing her trail. About ten miles north of Seattle we hit a clear stretch of freeway with an exit ramp at the far end. She turned off the exit ramp and pulled onto the shoulder. Any car that followed her off the ramp was burned. Those that went by would be watched. She would sit there for five minutes studying cars. A good rabbit has a good memory; I went on by. I wasn't burned but I'd have to watch the use of my Fiat. The day wasn't completely lost. I had a house and the source.

The source of Hammond's smuggling activities was Canada. From Canada would come the heroin that interested Sam's boys. From Canada would come decoy-flowers-China. There were two ways of likely entry: Vancouver or Victoria. Leanne could have been running a check on an automobile round trip from Vancouver. Or she could have been thinking of a round trip via Victoria and the ferry to Port Angeles, car to Winslow and ferry again to Seattle.

Leanne's little trick would work against anyone working alone. Either Pamela or myself working alone would be burned. But the Feds, if they were on to her and they were, would replace burned bodies with fresh ones. They would have at least two cars behind her and one in front—all with radios and fun codes.

And more in reserve.

I headed back to Seattle. She wasn't making her run today and I had enough for my pitch to the federal people. I drove to the Federal Building in downtown Seattle. The room number of the FBI was posted inside the elevators along with the rest of the government agencies. A couple of floors and I was there. I stepped through a frosted glass door and a diminutive secretary looked up. She was sitting behind a gray metal desk with a green top. Her electric typewriter looked bigger than she was.

"Yes, sir, may I help you?"

"Clint Johns, please, or Tony Butterfield."

"Just one moment, please. Whom shall I say is calling?"

"John Denson, captain of the dart squad."

If the secretary could have raised her eyebrows like Pamela Yew, she would have. As it is, she gave me what I can only describe as a look. She had rich auburn hair, stunning legs, and a knockout figure. She wasn't stupid. She had been condemned to being a secretary because of her sex. She knew that. I knew that. I smirked.

She smiled. "I don't think you're any such thing."

I shrugged. "I try. I'd sure like to be." She couldn't have been five feet tall. I wondered if she could sit in a regulation government swivel chair and touch the floor with her feet. I guessed not. "I don't imagine you're all that hot about being a secretary either; we all have our dreams."

She looked up at me with green eyes. "It's bad enough being a woman. When you're four foot eleven it's worse, somehow."

"I'm tired of being pursued for my body and not for my brains."

"You may go right on in, Mr. Denson."

I went in and there sat Johns, sans hat, behind a gray metal desk with a green top, just like his redheaded secretary.

"Hello, Denson. I see your throat's still intact."

"Getting in some report writing?"

Johns gave me a sour look. For every hour he spent in the field he probably spent three telling about it on government forms. There are right ways and wrong ways to write an agent's

144

report, an AR in the biz. AR's in bad form are not accepted; they must be rewritten.

"You and your girlfriend are going to get hurt if you keep nosing around in this business. Don't blame us if you do."

I wondered if the little redhead was Wayne Phillips's source. If she was, I envied him. "I was wondering if you people would be willing to arrange a little quid pro quo."

Johns shook his head. "Friend, you don't know a thing that's going on."

I told him what I'd learned from Phillips without telling him where I'd gotten it.

"Where did you learn all that?"

"Sleuthing," I said. "Holmesian deductions."

"Bullshit."

"Aren't you curious about what else I can supply?"

"What else?"

"Maybe the name of the ship the stuff's coming in on."

Johns looked like he didn't give a damn. "What is it?" he asked casually.

"I said maybe. It depends."

"On what?" Johns leaned forward in his government swivel chair.

"On me trailing along when you tail the run. You want the stuff. You want Hammond in the slammer. You want the Seattle Chinese out of the weeds. I want to make sure the Armstrong twins don't get their throats cut once Hammond thinks he's got everything he wants."

Johns considered that. "I don't know," he said.

"I also want a newspaper reporter friend of mine to make the run with me."

"That's out."

"Wayne Phillips of the *Star*. He won't write a word until you nail Hammond and flush the Chinese. After that, you and Butterfield are heroes. There's no way he can write a yarn with real drama unless he's there. Stuff for the movies." I leaned back and squinted my eyes. "I see Robert Redford as you."

"No."

"You bargain or you miss the boat."

"That won't happen."

"What makes you so sure? How about Paul Newman? I see Paul Newman as you."

He didn't say anything. Then no, again.

"If I know there's a multimillion dollar wad of heroin due to be smuggled in from Canada, other people surely know. What if you screw up? What if Hammond pulls it off? Good copy!"

Johns knew what I said was true. He didn't like it. "I'll have you in the pen, Denson. No deals. You'll tell me what you know. If I don't find out from you, I'll find out from your lady friend."

"Oh?" I leaned back in my chair. "Well, good luck, chum."

"You'll tell me what you know, Denson."

"I didn't say I knew. I said I might be able to help you. Then again I might not. It all depends."

"On what?"

"Lots of things. For starters, lay off Pamela Yew."

"Slick company, Denson."

"Adios, pal." I turned to leave.

"Done," he said behind my back.

I half turned. "Done what? Spell it out so I can be sure."

Johns doodled on a yellow legal pad with a felt-tipped pen. This was a business he didn't like, but he didn't have a choice. "You give me the specifics and I'll see to it that you and your scribbler friend are left alone. You and Hammond can wear the same pair of shorts across the line for all I care. But when we have to move we're gonna move fast. Just don't get in the way."

I smiled. "Fair enough. The *Hashita Maru*. Japanese registry. Out of Hong Kong and Singapore. Textiles this way. Lumber on the way back."

"How did you come by that?" Johns was depressed.

"They'll be making the run tomorrow, then?" I asked.

"Looks like it."

"How long has Leanne been practicing the run?"

"Once or twice a week earlier this fall. Then there was a break of a month or so when Hammond's flunkies went to

146

ground and took Leanne with them. This one this morning was the first one since then."

"You follow her every trip?"

"Every one, including the ones she doesn't complete."

"Every one?"

"We wait and watch."

"What happened today?"

"I got a call just a few minutes ago. She turned around a few miles from the Canadian border and is on her way back to Seattle."

"She's gotta know you're back there. Slick."

Johns let out a lungful of air through puffed cheeks. "That's the crazy part of the whole routine."

"You saw me and my trusty Fiat?"

"Sure."

"And she went through that little maneuver as one of her games."

"As near as we can figure out."

"Does Leanne have any choice in the matter?"

Johns looked at me. "We don't think so. Hammond has her hooked on dope, pounds on her regularly, and holds her twin sister hostage in that drinkwater home town of yours. He's not about to risk his ass on the run. Guys like Hammond don't think that way."

"You must think he can pull it off."

"That, friend, is precisely what bothers us. We can't figure it out."

"Does she come back down the Interstate or through Victoria and the ferry to Port Angeles?"

"The latter. When she makes the full circuit she always spends a night in Victoria. The hell of it is, Denson, most of the time she's empty. We don't know when she's loaded and when she isn't."

"Last summer, when you thought she might have been loaded, did she pick up the stuff in Vancouver?"

"As near as we can figure out."

"Why didn't you grab the stuff there?"

"Vancouver is in Canada. That's Canadian business. The

147

Canadians had their best people crawling all over the docks and had her Porsche under constant tail but she still managed to make the pickup. Nothing like this bundle coming up, mind you, but she still brought stuff across."

"It should be a simple matter to dismantle her little Porsche at Customs. Give those Port Angeles people a little excitement."

"Listen, last summer when they were making smaller runs, she did the same damned thing. Made the same trip again and again for weeks. Every week, almost, we stripped her little Porsche. It must have been tiresome as hell for her. For us it was even worse."

"Besides that you want the Chinese. If you scuttle this one too soon they'll stay in the weeds and bide their time."

"That's it. Hammond's a clever jerk who's in over his head. He wants to eliminate the Seattle terminal. If we run across the stuff at the border we plan to let it pass and keep an eye on it. But we've got to be sure we know where the stuff is. If we lose it and it hits the market, it's our rear."

"Phillips and I won't be in your way. What ferry does she take to Port Angeles?"

"When she makes the full run she's consistent. The eleven o'clock Red Ball Ferry, always."

"I think Phillips and I will go on ahead to Victoria tomorrow. Do a little drinking in The Reading Room bar at the Empress. We wouldn't want to miss the Red Ball and all of the excitement."

"Would you like a little spending money too? And maybe a girl to make your journey more pleasant?"

"Listen, about that girl, Sally . . ." I didn't know what to say next. It wasn't easy, since I had a good idea she was recruited by Clint Johns to help pin the guy who murdered her brother.

Johns looked at the top of his desk. "We used her as bait." He was barely audible. He moved a pile of forms on his desk.

"I'm very sorry about her," I said. "She was an awfully nice girl. Bright, and a good dancer."

Johns looked at the top of his desk. "We had her wired. We almost had a case against Hammond, almost but not quite. If he'd have talked to her we'd have had him in the pen by now."

He was barely audible. He moved a pile of forms on his desk. "What went wrong?"

Johns clenched his teeth together so tightly I could see the muscles of his jaws working. "We had a man asleep at the switch. We don't know what went wrong, for sure. All we know is Hammond got into the girl's dressing room without us seeing him and out again without us having any proof he was there."

"I thought you said you had her wired?"

"We did. We got her conversation with you and Pamela Yew after her dance. That's why we followed you here in Seattle. We had to make sure you weren't working with Hammond in some way."

"Didn't he say anything before he killed her. You can run a voice print."

Johns looked at the top of his desk. "He said nothing, Denson."

"Nothing?"

He shook his head. "Nothing. The girl sucked in her breath, apparently from recognizing him, and she was gone."

"That's it?"

"That's all. She should still be up at the university. We took advantage of her. It cost her life."

"So you can understand my concern about the twins, even if they are a little fouled up."

"I can. And Pamela Yew also."

"Pamela Yew can take care of herself."

"She's still a woman."

I laughed. "I want you guys to do a job, believe me. If Hammond thinks he's blown it, he may start drawing blood for the hell of it."

"That's crossed our minds more than once."

"How many men will you have working with you?"

"An army, Denson. Canadians and Americans."

The FBI had caught heroin smugglers before. But it's not every day that they'll agree to let an amateur risk her life to help them out. That's what they had done in Cayuse. A young man named Jimmy Whipple had been murdered by Hammond.

Johns had talked Jimmy's sister, Sally, into posing as a stripper in a ploy to trap Hammond. Sally Whipple wound up dead.

Clint Johns wanted Hammond.

I left Johns sitting there wishing he had done something else with his law degree.

Fourteen

I HAD TO FIGURE OUT Linda's cryptic reference to a decoy: ducks-decoys-flowers-China. Whatever that meant, I was sure it would put me further in front of Pamela Yew; I'd need every advantage I could get if I was to hold onto my Eakins. That's not to mention the possibility of some money involved. I couldn't imagine Pamela going to all this trouble unless there was a real payoff at the end. Sometimes the best place for me to solve puzzles is a bar. Not every bar. I headed for Pig's Alley and some draught Olympia. I took along a small head of cauliflower and cornered a salt shaker at the bar.

The Pig's was deserted except for a tall black man trying to talk to a young man at the bar. The black man was so drunk he was unintelligible. The young man grinned and nodded his head yes; he didn't know what the black man was saying. Finally, the young man moved down the bar to extricate himself from the situation. The black man turned his attention to me. He had a long, wrinkled face with large bags under yellow eyes. He spit some tobacco juice into a paper cup on the bar and cleared his throat. He said something about a baseball game, third base, and maybe a train; I couldn't be sure. He wavered on the bar stool and held an arm in my direction. A long hand drooped from the end of the arm. The fingers looked like sodden purple ropes.

"And he said 'you.' He was talking to me. And I said 'hey!'," the black man said. He looked at me with eyes that didn't focus. "Third base then, ya know. Good arm. Good bat. Had range. Lean." He blinked his eyes and rubbed them with the knuckles of his left hand. He took a drink of wine and looked at me. Did I understand? the yellow eyes asked.

"I can see it," I said. I couldn't but I wanted to. I wanted to know his story.

"He was from the big leagues. Big boys. He knew. He knew. And watched on Sundays." The black man's eyes began to water. "He knew his stuff. We coulda played. We coulda."

He was probably a better third baseman than anybody in the majors and a scout who couldn't sign him had told him that. "I know that. Everybody knows that," I said.

"We was good."

"You were damned good. I don't think there's any question about that now."

He was incapable of telling a coherent story because of the booze. He could only salvage bits and pieces and hope I was smart enough to catch on. Maybe the injustice of the past and the booze had isolated him permanently so that he was doomed to live out his life retelling the story of the Big League Scout. He had, no doubt, been a helluva third baseman. I could see him in his prime—tall, ebony black, and graceful.

"Listen, man, how about another wine?" I offered. It was a signal that I wanted off the hook and he knew it. He had told his story hundreds of times before.

"Just a second and I'll be finished. Only a minute. Always hoped, you know. Lots of us like that. Damned good."

"You should have been in the big leagues."

"Thanks, man," he said. He squeezed my shoulder.

"I understand," I said and squeezed his bony shoulder in return. I ordered another wine for him. The bartender stacked them two deep.

The black man turned and stared at the bar. Someone had listened at last. He was reviewing the story in his mind, remembering. He finished his wine while I stared out of the window at the Sound. In twenty minutes the black man was replaced by another elderly inhabitant of Skid Row.

I stood up. "Will you excuse me, please. I think I better be going now."

"Certainly," he said. I think he'd seen me with the ball player. He was disappointed at losing a source of freebie wine but he still had pride.

I left. I was drunk. The clock on the wall said it was one-thirty a.m. It was raining again. A cold rain. I didn't know what to do.

Question: Was Pamela Yew what she said she was? Yes.

Question: What was Pamela Yew after? Thing mineral, which, given her background as an artist, must be a work of art. The Jay Hamarr story was a nice gambit to get her into Cayuse and in the vicinity of Jerry Hammond. But you can fool all of the people some of the time, some of the people all of the time, and etc.

Question: Would Jerry Hammond continue to smuggle dope, knowing full well the federal government was watching his every move? No.

Question: Would the federal government really believe Jerry Hammond was as stupid as he appeared by his continued rehearsal of a smuggling run? Certainly. The federal government is capable of stupidity bordering on the absurd.

Question: If Jerry Hammond wasn't smuggling dope, then what was he smuggling? Thing mineral.

Question: If Jerry Hammond had really wanted to cut my throat that night on Hunt's Road, would he have failed? No. The affair on Hunt's Road just didn't figure. So what if he was wearing cowboy boots and I was wearing my fancy Nikes. He was fast and mean. I was a shrugger and a smirker, an indecisive twitch artist and a hopper. He couldn't have been half trying, which meant he really didn't want to cut me up. He only wanted to scare the hell out of me and wanted to make it look convincing.

Question: Why? I fitted into his plans somehow.

Question: What was the key? Decoy, without a doubt.

153

I remembered the story of a young man who rode a bicycle across the border every day. The Customs people knew he was smuggling something but they didn't know what. Day after day they tore his bicycle apart trying to figure it out. Finally they gave up and the chief customs officer took the young man aside. The officer told him they knew he was a smuggler but they just couldn't figure out what it was that he was smuggling. They were going to have to stop him from crossing at all. Just tell them what it was, he said, and they would forget the whole thing. He could cross but the smuggling was out.

"Bicycles," the young man replied.

That story was a version of Edgar Allen Poe's "The Purloined Letter" in which French detectives tore a house apart looking for an incriminating letter. The letter, which they couldn't find, was in a desk where the man kept his correspondence.

Jerry Hammond wasn't smuggling automobiles down from Canada. I didn't think he was smuggling heroin either. He was smuggling thing mineral, which must be valuable indeed.

Question: What would be the safest of all ways to smuggle thing mineral across the border? Have the government do it. If not the government, then John Denson, who was working with the government.

Let the government and me believe the moment had come at last for the Great Heroin Smuggling Run of All Time, Friends. And then, when all the government agents had assembled like extras in a Cecil DeMille movie, with John Denson among them sweating in confusion, Jerry Hammond would plant thing mineral in my Fiat.

The decoy?

Leanne Armstrong was the decoy. She was a decoy first for the federal government and now me. Sullivan would have laughed his rear off, seeing me suckered like that. When Leanne and her pals bolted, Jerry Hammond wanted them in the worst way; they were, after all, trying to screw him out of a fortune. When he couldn't find them he figured I could. He believed in specialists. He was a professional hit man. I was a professional at finding people. He must have gotten the idea at Sandy

154

Johnson's. My willingness to get my face kicked in for what must have seemed to him an odd sense of honor pegged me as a jerk. He was right on that one. I could be made to ignore common sense. He must also have known that Sally Whipple was a decoy working for the government. Who else but an FBI administrator would be dumb enough to have a college girl pose as a stripper in a honky-tonk bar? By slitting her throat he accomplished two things: he taught the government a thing or two and he gave me the incentive to stay on the trail of Leanne until I found her.

He laid a hell of a spread, the bastard. But I was onto him now. I knew the shot-at, the shooters, and the dekes. If I was right maybe I had an edge.

No, Pamela Yew had the edge. Hammond hadn't seen her when she delivered her kick at Sandy Johnson's. He assumed his assailant was a man. He assumed only men were his equal; women were to be pushed around.

I was just a half block from my Fiat when I met a naked man standing on the corner. I had run across a lot of strange things in cities but he was my first naked man. He was just standing there in the rain, watching the neon lights flicker and blink up the street. He was middle-aged with white skin and a stomach that sagged low over his privates. He was neither handsome nor happy. The early morning traffic slowed on the street; people peered at him out of foggy windows. It was warm in their cars, what with the heaters. There wasn't anybody on the sidewalks. It was too wet. I decided the naked man needed to talk to someone.

He gave me an amiable smile when I walked up to him. We could have been members of an Elks convention, strangers, but members of the same fraternity.

"Got a match?" I asked. It was a stupid thing to ask of a naked man.

"Sorry, I don't smoke," he said. "Frank Broyhill." He extended a hand.

"John Denson." We shook.

"Hell of a night."

"Kind of wet out here," I said.

"Oh, I don't mind the rain."

"Waiting for anything in particular?" There are unspoken rules for the distance between two people in casual conversation. Latin Americans like to talk up close, beak to beak. North Americans like more distance. A Colombian will back a New Yorker into a corner at a cocktail party. There are no rules for chatting with a naked man in the rain on a street corner in Seattle.

"I'm waiting for my ship to come in," he said with an odd look in his eye.

"Well, I wish you luck."

His eyes were beginning to water. He was going to start weeping any second.

"See you around," I said. I strode off briskly in the direction of my Fiat. I had visions of a naked fat man on my back pummeling me, blaming me for a past gone wrong. I could hear the crazy boop, beep, boop, beep of a siren behind me. I didn't look back.

Fifteen

IT WAS THREE A.M. when I got home. I was still dizzy from the booze but I felt better. I knew about the decoy. Pamela Yew didn't. I called Wayne Phillips at his home.

"Hey, Wayne, this is John Denson."

"Christ's sakes, man, this is the middle of the night."

"Hammond will be making the run tomorrow. I want you to go with me to Victoria to spend the night."

"So why couldn't you tell me about it in the morning?"

"Ah," I laughed. "All kinds of reasons. What kind of car do you drive?"

"An old bug, got a hundred thousand on it."

"That's too bad. Tomorrow morning you'll either have to rent a red Fiat like mine or trade your Volkswagen in for one. I know a dealer who'll be able to give you a match."

"The hell you say!" Phillips was wide awake now. "What's the matter with my bug?"

"Do you want a story right out of 'The French Connection' dumped right in your lap?" What was a little bull between friends?

"The hell you say!"

"You said that already. I say again: You'll have to get a

157

Fiat identical to mine in the morning even if it means trading your Volkswagen."

"What for?"

"Tit for tat, Wayne. Decoy for decoy."

"Decoy?"

"Have you ever met Hammond?"

Phillips paused. "Never had the pleasure."

"See you in the morning," I said. "I'll come by early." I didn't give him a chance to answer. I hung up.

Wayne Phillips was drinking coffee and reading his own stories when I got to his place.

"Those morons will louse it up every time," he said without looking up from his newspaper. He took another sip of black coffee. "There's more coffee on the stove," he said.

I poured myself a cup and joined him at his kitchen table, which was sticky from unwashed grime. He pointed to one of his stories.

"They can't leave well enough alone. Always screwing over your copy. You'd think they'd have brains enough to check with the reporter. Sometimes we're rational. Sometimes we think. Now I'll have to answer phone calls from readers all morning wanting to know just how it was I balled up a few simple facts. And in a few days the letters to the editor will start coming in, pointing out in detail what I said in the first damned place!" Phillips was almost shouting. He glared at me.

"I believe you," I said. I took a sip of his awful coffee.

"Your friend Powell is one of the worst offenders."

"He's not a bad guy," I said.

Phillips looked at me. "Listen, Denson, he gets bored sitting there throwing away press releases so he starts messing with people's copy. The bastard never gets out of the city room!" Phillips was shouting again.

"Drink some more coffee," I said.

"That's the second time this week. The second time!"

"He means well."

"Maybe he means well enough but he and the rest of the morons who run that place have all these notions about how the world is supposed to be out there. By God if their reporters' copy doesn't fit, then they'll just change the copy. Simple as that! You can't blame the reader if he gets confused now and then."

"Did you spring some time off for our project?"

"I called Powell and told him I caught a social disease and decided to take a couple of days off so as not to spread it around the city room." Phillips grinned.

"What did he say?"

"I hung up before he could answer. Let's get going," he said and finished his coffee.

It took us almost two and a half hours to find a dealer with a Fiat like mine who was willing to rent it for a couple of days. Luck was with us.

"Now what?" asked Phillips.

"Easy. We separate for a litle trip to Victoria. You take the ferry to Winslow on the peninsula and drive north to Port Angeles. You take the ferry across the Straits of Juan de Fuca to Victoria."

"And you?"

"Me, I drive north on Interstate 5 and cross the border at Blaine. I take the Canadian Pacific ferry to Sydney on Vancouver Island and drive south to Victoria. You from the south by way of the Olympic Peninsula and the ferry north. Me from Canada and the ferry west."

"What happens after I get there?"

"You find someplace downtown to hide your car and you meet me at the Reading Room bar in the Empress Hotel late this afternoon."

Phillips shook his head. "Are you going to tell me what this is all about?"

I grinned. "If I tell you what's going on you'll start to think. You think too much and we're in trouble."

We parted. He for the ferry. Me for the interstate highway north, a three-hour drive to the Canadian border, and another hour-and-a-half ferry ride.

A few miles after the ferry landed at Sydney, I spotted Jerry Hammond sitting in his Mercury. He was parked in a gas station. I watched in my rearview mirror. Hammond pulled in behind me several cars later.

Jerry Hammond knew how to lay a spread. He had waited; he was patient. And here I came, just like he knew I would. He wouldn't have to eye me nervously for weeks with flowers-China on ice.

Phillips beat me to the Reading Room bar. He was drinking a bottle of Molson's Ale. It was one of the loveliest bars on the West Coast. From it you look out over some lovely grounds to Victoria's small harbor across the street. The harbor was filled with sailboats berthed side by side with commercial fishing boats and flanked on both sides by ferry terminals. It was a lovely scene and a beautiful afternoon.

I joined Phillips at the bar. "Have a nice trip?" I asked.

"Aw yeah, very nice," he said. He was drunk. "This's a helluva building, Denson. What kind of building is this anyway? It's incredible. Christ!" With a gesture of his hand he ordered another ale. "Gotta tell you, Denson, I like Canadian ale."

Just what I needed, an alcoholic newspaper reporter screwing things up. "I think it's called Mansard. I remember reading an aritcle about it in Sunset. The steep roofs are the key; the style dates from the seventeenth century. I don't want to nag you, Wayne, but I think it'd be a champion idea for you to lay off the booze until we see this thing through."

Phillips looked at me and grinned. "It is a helluva building. I've never missed a deadline on account of booze yet, pal. I may get a trifle blasted but I keep rolling."

I'll bet he had missed deadlines, but it was too late to worry then. "Can you skip the booze in the morning?"

"No Bloody Marys."

"No Bloody Marys, no quick shots of whiskey, no nothing."

"What the hell." He grinned, "I don't get rolling until one, two o'clock at least."

I looked at the sailboats in the small harbor and drifted off. "Well, I was right."

"About what?" Phillips looked confused.

"Hammond. He followed me down from Sydney. Thinks he's invisible or something."

"What if he comes in here and sees us drinking together?"

"Let him. No way he could be in two places at the same time. He couldn't possibly have seen you come in at the Red Ball terminal and me at Sydney within an hour of each other."

"So far as he knows there is only one Fiat in town like yours. That's the idea."

"If you did a job of hiding your rented number."

"I did a job," he said.

"We've got to lay our spread just so. Everything has to look okay or Hammond will bolt. If I've got it figured out right, Hammond will plant his payload on my Fiat tonight. He's out there right now, casing the parking lot. Tomorrow morning I get his attention. You switch Fiats, license plates, and the contents of the trunks. He watches me, the Customs people ignore me because I'm working for the federal people."

"He follows the decoy." Phillips grinned.

"Ah, you've got it. You turn my Fiat over to the Customs people and take notes while they strip it looking for heroin?"

Phillips loved it. "Hell of a story!"

"Only they won't find anything."

"Huh?"

"They won't find anything." I motioned to the bartender for another drink.

"Say that again. They won't what?"

"I said they won't find anything. There will be a painting in the trunk. While they're looking for heroin I want you to casually walk off with that painting."

"Casually walk off with it?"

"That's it."

Phillips didn't like what he was hearing. He narrowed his eyes. "Now just where is that story you promised me?"

"Good point there, Wayne. First of all you have to imagine the federal people swooping down on my Fiat like ten thousand wild Indians bearing down on General Custer. The big score at last and there you are, a member of the press, to record their heroic coup. Are you with me?"

161

Phillips shook his head. "You're sadistic."

"They can just see their names out there on page one. Promotions. Maybe a personal commendation from the Director. They'll want to make sure you have their names spelled correctly. You'll have to be careful about their names. Make a big deal about correct spelling."

"Then nothing."

"Ah, you've got it." I laughed. "Nothing. Tens of thousands of taxpayers' dollars flushed down the toilet. Incompetent fools. And you've got every delicious little detail. Is that a story? The readers will love it. Suspicions verified."

Phillips slapped the bar with the palm of his hand and laughed. "Now you can tell me about this painting that I'm supposed to walk off with. I want to know everything you know."

"I think this heroin business is a decoy, an elaborate ruse by Hammond to divert attention from the painting. He's a smuggler and he's being watched. The painting's his big score. I think it's a masterpiece from Asia somewhere and Hammond doesn't want to be bothered with taxes and awkward questions."

"So I'm just supposed to walk off with it."

"That's it, Wayne. Pull it off and I'll give you ten percent of whatever I get out of it."

Phillips lifted his ale for a toast. "Better than a goddamned story any day of the week."

"I thought you'd feel that way." I felt good; I was one day away from the score and Pamela Yew was in Seattle.

"You don't have any idea what the damned thing looks like?"

"No idea. It might have some flowers in it, I don't know."

Sixteen

THE BARTENDER LEANED OVER the bar. "Excuse me, sir, I'm told your wife is waiting for you in the lobby."

I sat upright on the bar stool. "My wife?"

"Yes, sir, Mrs. Denson. She would like for you to help her with her bags."

Phillips looked bewildered. "Mrs. Denson? I didn't know you were married. Why are you dragging your wife along on this thing?"

My shoulders drooped. "She's not the type that likes to stay home and do the dishes." I got up and walked out to the lobby. There she was, surrounded by bellhops eager to be of service.

She spotted me and grinned. "John, darling, I thought I'd never find you. With these bags on the ferry and all it was just too much." It was too much at that. She ran for me with open arms, embraced me and planted a big kiss on my lips. "How are tricks, Mr. Denson?" she whispered in my ear.

"Pamela dear!" I gave her a passionate embrace as close as I could come to a public display of rape.

"Calm down," she hissed in my ear.

I let her go. "Isn't there any way I can get rid of you?"

She straightened her jacket. "A woman's place is at the side of her husband. Serving his every need."

"Okay, how did you get here?"

"I followed Hammond. I figured you have the skill to ditch me. He either didn't know or didn't care. He was like following a turkey through a supermarket."

"And your plan now?"

"Why, to stay by your side, Mr. Denson. I knew from the beginning it would be difficult to beat Jerry Hammond in Seattle. I don't have the contacts."

"But I do?"

"Yes, Mr. Denson, you do."

It was becoming clear to me; she was more subtle than I had supposed. "So you decided to use mine."

"That's exactly what I decided. The trick was to get you interested in thing mineral without knowing what it was."

"You're not gonna tell me you decided on this jackass bet from the beginning."

Pamela Yew laughed. "No, I'm not going to tell you that. I had no idea you had an Eakins on your wall. What I do know about is the male ego. I knew you'd be romantic enough to believe that nonsense about Jay Hamarr. I also knew sooner or later you'd find out the truth about Bobby Carroll. I knew, Mr. Denson, that you'd want to show me a thing or two about being a detective. I knew you'd do precisely what you're trying to do now."

"You knew that."

"Oh, yes, I knew that. All I've had to do, Mr. Denson, is stay with you, let you do the work. I'll make book you don't have any real idea what thing mineral is. I do." She raised her hand and signaled to a bellhop. "Our room number, Mr. Denson?"

I gave her my room number. "The very least you could do for this imposition is to buy me dinner."

Pamela Yew kissed me on the forehead. "Certainly, I always pay my own way. After all, you rented the room; I'll spring for dinner."

"I like prime rib."

"Ah," she waved expansively. "Prime rib it is. No husband of mine eats hamburger."

Pamela Yew sat up in my room after dinner, reading a

paperback novel. I descended to the Reading Room bar and drank overpriced martinis. I wondered just how in the hell it was that I'd gotten myself in such a jam. There she was, ersatz Mrs. John Denson, lying there in my bed reading a book. At eleven o'clock I returned to my room to go to bed. She kept her distance on the far side of the Queen-sized bed. She didn't say anything while I brushed my teeth.

I slipped into bed and there was a silence. "Someday you might want to tell me how you got into the hooker business," I said.

"What?"

"You choose the time. Whenever you think is right?"

She said nothing.

"My bet your eye has something to do with it. You don't have a sister."

She looked at me cautiously. "I drew a mean pimp, Mr. Denson. Cost me eighty percent vision in this eye. I got a fractured jaw, some broken teeth and this."

"A mashed face."

"It was only my third week and I had a disagreement with my pimp. You remember the photograph of that girl I showed you?"

I nodded yes.

"Well, my face looked like that. They wouldn't let me look in a mirror for two weeks. When they did I started crying and couldn't stop. I wept until I was weak. Nobody wanted to be near me, I was so ugly; it was like I had cancer or something."

"I don't know what to say."

"You don't have to say a thing, Mr. Denson. It hurts to tell a story like that; it hurts to hear one."

"I'm very, very sorry, Pamela."

"Good night, Mr. Denson."

"Good night, Ms. Yew."

Wayne Phillips got up at seven a.m. and checked out, leaving by the front of the hotel. A half-hour later, I dragged myself out of bed and competed with Pamela Yew for space in the bathroom. After we were dressed I retreated to the hall, Pamela

165

by my side, and found a window overlooking the large parking lot at the rear of the Empress. I squatted by the window with my companion pressed against me trying to see what I was looking at.

Hammond would be out there. He would be loath to take his eye off my Fiat even for a second.

He hadn't taken much pain to hide. He had grabbed an on-street parking spot earlier in the morning and was inside his Lincoln reading a newspaper.

His spread was laid just right, the dekes set just so, facing into the wind. If I spotted him there it would make no difference. Better to keep an eye on me. Right? Wrong.

I had some breakfast and took a stroll with my new wife across the street to buy a ticket to Port Angeles at the Red Ball terminal.

"This is dutch, love," I told Pamela.

"Certainly," she said.

The girl at the window said the ferry would leave at eleven o'clock.

"First come, first serve," she asid.

"What if I'm a bit late?"

"Management doesn't guarantee a ride with a ticket, sir."

I was back in my room by nine, waiting. So was Pamela Yew. She knew I wouldn't try to strong-arm her to win a bet. A few minutes later the phone rang.

Wayne Phillips. "It's me, John, have you spotted him?"

"Just a second, Wayne," I leaned over and turned on the radio full blast and spoke softly into the receiver. "He's being brash as hell. Sitting in a Lincoln watching the lot from the street."

"What do we do now?"

"We time it for nine thirty on the nose. You better be a fast man with a screwdriver."

Pamela Yew leaned forward. She didn't know what he was talking about but was aware that a $50,000 Thomas Eakins was on the line.

"I'll do my best," said Phillips.

I looked at Pamela. "All right, Wayne, at nine twenty-five

I'll walk out the back door with my overnight bag and my wife's luggage. I'll look around and spot Hammond. I'll throw my overnight bag in the back seat and my wife and I will walk over to his car and keep him busy for ten minutes. My wife understands the stakes. That's all the time you'll need. Don't forget to keep the luggage in the right Fiat."

"What if the parking attendant gets curious?"

"Buy him off, I don't care. Just ten minutes, that's all."

"Oh boy!"

"There's an FBI agent in Bremerton named Charlie Grisdale. The FBI will know about today's run. Call him. He'll meet you at Customs." I gave Pamela Yew a smile. "Tell him what happened. Tell him we only had a hunch, nothing more, or we would have told Johns."

"What? Why don't you turn the damned radio down?"

"Got that?"

"I think so. Is this guy Grisdale an okay guy?"

"No sweat. Wait for the three o'clock ferry, now. Don't jump the gun."

"The three o'clock. Done. Why the radio?"

"My wife's a gossip," I said and hung up.

The Yew eyebrow went up. "Oh, you're so suspicious, Mr. Denson. Are you trying to get me to follow your friend, is that it?"

I shrugged. "I don't know."

She smiled. "I'll follow you. You want to tell me what thing mineral is?"

"No."

She laughed. "I didn't think so. May the best person win."

"Whatever. Since I'm stuck with you, I'll have to have your help with at least part of my plan or neither of us will have a shot at thing mineral. You get my drift?"

"I think so."

"At nine thirty the two of us have got to take a stroll back of the Empress here and distract Hammond's attention for maybe ten minutes."

Pamela Yew raised both eyebrows. "Oh, why is that, Mr. Denson?"

167

I grinned and shook my head. "That I don't tell you."

"Oh!"

"Do I have your word?"

She didn't have any other choice. "You've got it."

"Hammond is sitting back there in his Lincoln. I want you to dazzle him with your charm while I let the air out of one of his tires. He won't do anything. He'll sit right there and take it, believe me."

"Done," she said.

By nine fifteen my hands began to shake a trifle. Nerve time. Truth time. Time to set my decoys. I got up with a knot in the pit of my stomach. With Pamela Yew clinging to my arm like a woman in a soap opera, I took a stroll through the Empress Hotel's lovely halls to the back door and the parking lot. I walked over to my car. My watch said it was 9:27. I turned and walked directly to Hammond's Lincoln, a matter of maybe forty yards.

"Is this some kind of fertility rite?" asked Pamela.

"Just keep your end of the bargain."

"I will, Mr. Denson."

Hammond put down his newspaper and watched us approach him without saying a word. There was a lot of traffic on the street; I was thankful for that.

I walked casually around the Lincoln and squatted in front of the left rear tire—on the traffic side.

Hammond rolled down his window.

Pamela Yew stood just beyond his reach, plunged her hand down in front of her blouse and began tugging at her bra. "Got a little bind," she said.

Hammond glanced quickly from me to her and back to me again. "What the fuck are you doing?"

"I can't answer for Pamela but I'm letting the air out of your tire. I don't like people following me around."

Hammond couldn't risk retaliating and having the police drag him out of sight of my Fiat. "Get the hell away from there!" he yelled.

"Haven't you got that thing fixed yet?" I said to Pamela.

She looked concerned. "Too much breast, not enough bra."

Hammond stared at her.

I started giggling.

Pamela looked innocently at Hammond. "You look surprised at my chest, sir. Don't you know about women's bosoms? I'm told men admire them."

Hammond twisted violently in his seat. He was surrounded by people on the sidewalks and in the street. "Listen, Denson, get away from my tire," he yelled at me.

"What are you going to do, cut my throat?" I asked mildly.

Pamela, finished with her front, now hiked her skirt up and began examining her thigh.

"Now what are you up to, bitch?"

Pamela looked surprised. "I've got a little itch here," she said. She began scratching her thigh. The insanity of the scene had gotten to her, though, and she couldn't remain serious any longer. She dropped her skirt and began to giggle at Hammond.

All three of us could hear the air racing from the tire. "It's convenient finding you here, Mr. Hammond," I said. "But whatever it is you're smuggling to Seattle in Leanne Armstrong's car I'm gonna beat you to it. You might say I'm riding shotgun on this little trip."

"Regular old cowboy," Hammond said.

Pamela Yew watched me carefully. Was it possible to fake both of them at once? "Regular old cowboy," I said.

"My book says you're chickenshit, Denson."

I shrugged. "You're losing all your air there, friend."

"It'll fix. You two just stay out of my way this afternoon. I got enough to worry about as it is."

"We're going to be right behind that girl's car all the way to Seattle. At least I am. I can't speak for Ms. Yew here."

"Oh yes, I'll be there too," Pamela said.

"You stay out of my way, pal."

"Okay," I said casually. Phillips's time was up. "My dear," I gestured to Pamela with my arm.

"At your side, Mr. Denson." She joined me for the walk back to the Empress Hotel. "What was that little charade all about?" she asked.

"Just funnin' a redneck a trifle."

"I don't think so." She looked back as Hammond scrambled to his trunk to get his spare. I tried the key Phillips had given me to his rented Fiat. It turned. Only the license plates were mine. Wayne Phillips, a fast man with a screwdriver, was off with my Fiat. Unless I was dreadfully wrong, in the trunk of that Fiat was thing mineral. Hammond was a fast man with a flat. He had it changed by the time I paid my bill in the Empress and returned with Pamela Yew clinging to my arm. Ms. Yew said nothing.

"A penny for your thoughts, good wife?"

"I think I may have been finessed."

"No finesse. As you probably suspect, thing mineral is in the trunk of Leanne Armstrong's automobile. What it boils down to is that I have to beat you and Hammond into that trunk or I lose my Eakins."

Pamela wasn't convinced. "What about the Customs people?"

"The Customs people think he's smuggling heroin."

"Oh?"

Hammond was only five cars behind me in the line at the Red Ball terminal. Pamela was quiet, figuring the angles, but I didn't think she was onto me yet.

"You didn't tell me about that phone call you received this morning, Mr. Denson?" she asked.

"No."

"I don't imagine you're going to, either."

"No," I said again.

Leanne didn't leave her Porsche once during the hour-and-a-half ride from Victoria to Port Angeles. Hammond stayed in his Lincoln. Pamela Yew stayed in the rented Fiat watching Leanne. It was a good thing we had taken her BMW to Cayuse. She had never seen the inside of my Fiat. I went upstairs, read the papers, and had clam chowder served in a paper bowl. It wasn't bad chowder.

When the loudspeaker asked us to return to our cars, I descended the stairs from the passenger's cabin with a knot in my stomach. It was time for the last act: I still wasn't certain if I had read Hammond's decoys right.

"Did I lose my painting, Mr. Denson?" Pamela asked when the front of the ferry parted and the automobiles disgorged.

"As I understand it I have to have thing mineral in hand before I win."

"That's it."

"Then I haven't won yet."

"But you expect to."

"Yes," I said. "I expect to."

Seventeen

IT WAS RAINING SLIGHTLY in Port Angeles. There seemed to be more than the usual number of uniformed Customs officials on hand. There was a clear reason that would irritate an awful lot of ferry-goers.

There were to be six checking stations open to handle the ferry traffic that day. However, only four of those were open for business as usual; lanes one and two were abbreviated. Hammond and his Lincoln were put at the head of lane one. Leanne and her Porsche led the parade at lane two. My Fiat was cut out of the confusion and placed directly behind the Porsche.

I read the sports pages of the Victoria newspaper while the puzzled Customs people searched. And searched. And searched. Their plodding effort turned slightly manic in the end but they struggled to remain calm.

"Do you really think they'll let thing mineral pass, Mr. Denson?"

"Sure of it, love."

"I don't think it's in the trunk of Leanne's Porsche."

"Oh!" I looked surprised. "Where do you think it is?"

She smiled. "I think Jerry Hammond planted it in the trunk

172

of this car. I think your newspaper friend checked to make sure while we let the air out of Hammond's car."

She was clairvoyant. Almost. "Why would Hammond plant thing mineral in my car?"

"Because it will make it through Customs in your car but not his. He's keeping his eye on this car, not Leanne's."

She was still a half step behind. "Why will it make it through in my car and not his? I don't understand."

Pamela Yew fingered the elaborate pendant she wore around her throat. "Because, Mr. Denson, you gave the federal people some information they didn't have. You connived your way along out of your great concern for the Armstrong twins. I bet when your turn comes they'll give a perfunctory glance through the window and wave you on. One of the boys. Then, voila! You'll produce thing mineral, providing Hammond doesn't take it away from you. May I look in your trunk?"

I looked at her blandly. "I don't think so."

"No?"

"Fun watching you sweat, Ms. Yew. Thing mineral's in the trunk of that Porsche up ahead."

"You must like your trunk a lot. I noted you put our bags in the back seat."

"Habit, nothing more. Easy to fling 'em in the back seat."

At last the Customs people made the decision to reassemble the mess they had made out of the Lincoln and the Porsche. The agents didn't behave like government employees who were given a big assignment and were successful. No, they looked more like bureaucrats who had muffed it and were running scared. Had they overlooked something?

There had to be heroin there somewhere. Their superiors had said so.

When our turn came in the lane the young lady gave me a cheery smile and waved me on my way. Butterfield and Johns were living up to their end of the bargain.

"You're going to have to arm-wrestle me to get thing mineral out of this car, Mr. Denson."

"I don't have to muscle you to win this one. The action's all up here." I tapped the side of my head with my finger.

173

"If you win, I hope you're not all brain and nothing else, Mr. Denson."

I leered at her and pulled in behind Leanne's Porsche for the drive to Winslow and the ferry to Seattle. The sooner I got Hammond and Pamela Yew to Seattle, the quicker Wayne Phillips could return my luggage and thing mineral to my apartment.

It was late in the afternoon when we arrived in Winslow to join the line for the ferry. The weather had taken a turn for the worse. The light rain turned to fog, then back to rain again. It was wet, cold and depressing.

We waited, my Fiat idling with the heater on. I watched the head of the line for any sign the cars were beginning to move.

"Mr. Denson?"

I turned to face the muzzle of Pamela Yew's pearl-handled .38. "Whoa," I said.

"It's time, Mr. Denson."

"Time for what?" Neither her hand nor her eyes betrayed any hesitation.

"Time to look in the trunk of your car to see if you in fact have thing mineral."

"If you think I'm going to pay off on a bet won at the bad end of that thing you're a whole lot mistaken."

Pamela Yew laughed. "If you think I ever believed you'd go for a bet as preposterous as that you're equally mistaken, Mr. Denson. Out please, and let's check your trunk. It's that or you can start hoofing it for the ferry and leave me here with your car. Take your pick."

"Let's check the trunk."

"Let's."

She followed me to the trunk, holding her Beretta under a scarf draped over her hand. I opened the trunk.

Nothing.

"It's empty," said Pamela.

"I didn't expect to find much."

She put her pistol back in her handbag. "This car's a decoy."

"Uh huh, it sure is."

"Where's thing mineral?"

"Thing mineral's in my car. Hammond put it in there last night. A newspaper friend of mine switched the contents and cars this morning while we harassed Hammond on the street."

Pamela Yew whacked herself on the forehead with the heel of her hand: "Oh my God!"

"A clear winner," I said as I slipped back into the car.

"When I see thing mineral," she said.

"You're not giving up yet?"

"Not yet, Mr. Denson."

That left me wondering what could possibly have gone wrong. Pamela Yew sat placidly listening to the radio.

We were put aboard the ferry twenty minutes later. This time Leanne left her Porsche for the passenger's lounge upstairs. She looked back at me as she headed for the stairwell. I started to open the door but she shook her head no and disappeared into the crowd with a frightened look. The foghorn sounded.

"I think she might be in a whole lot of trouble, Pamela. I'm going up after her."

Pamela slipped her handbag over her shoulder. "I'm by your side, Mr. Denson."

We hadn't gotten more than twenty feet before we were stopped short by Jerry Hammond, drinking a can of Coca-Cola. He finished the dregs, crushed the can with his left hand, and walked straight at us.

"Afternoon, Denson," he said with a smile. "Ma'am." He made a slight bow toward Pamela.

"Nice day for a Coke," I said. "Pamela and I thought we'd have one."

"I'll be needing the keys to your little Fiat, Denson."

"We can give you a lift, wherever you want to go. We've got lots of time; isn't that right, Pamela?"

"He's right. Like he said, we've got lots of time. Wherever you want to go."

Hammond grinned at Pamela. "This morning when you two were hassling me in my car I wondered where I'd seen you before. I remember now."

"I can't imagine you'd forget," she said.

He laughed. "Oh, I'd forgotten okay. One woman here or

175

there, they come together in your mind after a while. You know how it is."

Pamela Yew didn't say anything. I was wondering what the connection was. I wanted to say something but it was Hammond's show.

"I bet you got a real thrill out of kicking me in the nuts the other day. I thought it was a man all along. Don't know what made me think that. Had to beat the truth out of the little wife."

"You won't be finding any dope in my Fiat," I said.

Hammond was amused. "You're old enough, Denson. You ever watch the Green Bay Packers when Bart Starr was quarterback?"

"Saw 'em on the tube."

"Then you gotta remember how old Bart'd get 'em third and inches and the Bears or Giants or whoever would put eleven of the biggest, meanest suckers you ever saw up there on the line to stop Jimmy Taylor from ripping up the gut."

"I remember."

Hammond grinned. "Then old Bart'd drop back and loft one to Boyd Dowler or Max McGee for six. Did it all the time."

"So?"

"So I lofted one. There ain't no dope in that trunk."

Thing mineral. I glanced at Pamela Yew. "What is in the trunk?"

"Don't make no sense to jaw about that now. It's time for the carving."

"Carving?"

"Why yes, you and the pretty lady."

I never was an especially good poker player. My trump was the fact that thing mineral was not in the Fiat on board the ferry at all. Thing mineral was in my Fiat safe in the hands of Wayne Phillips.

That was my trump but I didn't play it. All I had to do was tell him. I didn't. I had Leanne Armstrong to think of as well as Pamela Yew and myself.

"A ferry's a mighty small place, Denson."

He started coming for us.

"A fine and private place," I said. A hell of a time to remember an English poet. I started looking for a way out. I wasn't thinking all that clearly. I started backing as I looked. I held onto Pamela's elbow as I backed.

"I think we're in trouble, Mr. Denson. I might need to use that elbow."

I let go of her elbow. "I think you may be right."

"You two ain't going nowhere. I told you that out on the road the other night." Hammond was a real charmer.

The heels of his fancy cowboy boots echoed on the rough wood of the deck.

"You meet all kinds of people on a ferry," said Pamela.

The heels kept coming. I hoped Pamela and I didn't trip over one another.

"Now listen, dammit," I said.

Hammond kept coming. I started trying car doors with the idea of locking Pamela and myself inside somebody's Ford. Pamela moved quietly by my side. Hammond grinned as I tried door handles. He could see, as Pamela and I could, the large signs, on both sides of the deck, which informed the world that management was not responsible for theft. All car doors were to be locked when the passengers were topside. Pamela and I retreated down the deck. I felt reasonably safe there because many of the cars were occupied.

Then I saw it: a new Oldsmobile just two cars down. I could see a man in the front seat. A wife also. Both were leaned against the door, apparently asleep. There was a daughter in the back seat reading a paperback novel.

Pamela Yew saw it also. "Our salvation, Mr. Denson?"

"I hope so." I rapped on the windshield; the father awoke with a start. The girl put down her paperback in the back seat. It was *The Territorial Imperative*, by Robert Ardrey. Man as an animal and all that. It was hard for me to believe she was reading that book.

"This man here, he's trying to kill us." I motioned to Hammond.

"He's right," said Pamela Yew.

Hammond grinned pleasantly.

"Please let us in," I said.

177

"He's trying to kill us," said Pamela.

"He's got a knife," I said.

Hammond looked hurt and surprised. He held his hands out so the driver could see they were empty. He had an easy, down-home smile.

"I'm telling you the truth," I persisted.

The driver stared up blankly at me. He looked at Pamela, then at his wife. She concluded we were screwballs, Californians maybe.

"At least honk your horn so we can get some help," Pamela asked.

"No," said the driver. He didn't want to embarrass himself by honking his horn on a ferry, even if it cost the lives of two people. His wife was speaking to the back of his head in low and hurried tones. Neither Pamela nor I could hear what the wife said.

We weren't much smarter than they were. We should have stayed right there but we didn't. We started to back off. Rather than create an embarrassing scene we would let Hammond have a go at us with his knife.

Hammond was in no hurry. He looked at the occupants in the front seat, then at us, and made a circling motion around his ear with his finger.

"A nutty couple. They love practical jokes," he said.

The daughter, who was a real beauty, watched us through the rear window.

The wife, I could see, was still giving her husband advice. She might as well be sticking a knife through my ribs and Pamela Yew's abdomen.

The driver looked back uncertainly.

Pamela Yew smiled pleasantly and gave him the bird finger.

That cracked me up. "My God, Ms. Yew, are we getting a bit looney?"

Pamela shrugged her shoulders as she retreated. "He can remember the bird when he reads our obits."

I tried to keep at least three cars between us and Hammond, just as I kept a nice distance between the two of us that night on Hunt's road. Hammond must have sensed what I was thinking.

"This ferry doesn't stretch clear across the state of Washington like that road; it's gotta end sometime."

I could see there were few if any passengers in their cars at that end of the deck, a perfect place for Hammond to do his business. I saw a stairway to the upstairs deck to my left; I motioned to it with my eyes and Pamela picked up the cue. She started angling for it. Hammond saw it too and began moving quickly to cut us off.

I tripped over a trailer hitch and suddenly he was bending over me with his knife at my throat.

"Get the hell out of here," I yelled at Pamela Yew.

She stayed.

"You want me to cut you up now or would you like a chance in the water?" He looked at Pamela. "You, Pamela whatever your name is. You come too."

"Name's Yew," I said.

"For God's sake, shut up, John," Pamela said. She stared at the knife.

"I could let a little blood now and take a chance dragging your stiffs to the railing. Or I could just leave you here. But those assholes in the Olds saw my face and I'd never make it off the ferry. Or you could both accompany me to the railing, friendly like, for a little swim. It's your only chance."

"We'll take it," said Pamela. She couldn't keep her eyes off the knife at my throat.

"We'll take the water," I said.

"Give me your car keys."

I gave him my car keys.

Hammond put the tip of his knife on my kidney. "Now you get to your feet, easy like, and remember: you even twitch and in it goes."

I got up, easy like, and the three of us began moving toward the stairwell. He had to reach the next deck to find a convenient place for the demise of John Denson and Pamela Yew. I looked back over my shoulder in the direction of the Oldsmobile. The daughter was reading her book again; the folks were asleep.

We met absolutely no one either on the way to the stairwell or going up the stairs. Once we were on deck there was only the fog.

All of the sudden we were at a railing. The Puget Sound slid by below us, cold and black.

There was no way out. I had to play my trump then, forget thing mineral and place our hides before Leanne Armstrong's.

"Listen, Hammond, there's something you should know. I pulled a little stunt on you in Victoria. I . . ."

Too late.

Hammond gave me his all-American grin as he pushed me overboard. He had beautiful teeth, Hammond. I had to give him that. And he kept his word about the knife.

The impact of the water knocked the wind out of me but I started swimming for all I was worth, air or no. The ferry's enormous screws would come slicing along momentarily. The foghorn blew ominously.

I missed the screws, thank God. Or they missed me. They missed Pamela Yew also. There she was, not fifteen feet away.

"Why didn't you use your damn weapon?"

"Me?"

"You!"

She didn't say anything. I suspected she'd never had to use it. "How long do we have?" she asked.

"At these temperatures a half-hour, maybe forty-five minutes."

"Truth time, John Denson?"

"Truth time, Pamela Yew."

She started to speak but was interrupted by the throb of a marine diesel. It seemed to have come from nowhere.

"Hey!" I yelled. "Hey, there! Help!"

"Stand fast and keep talking," came a voice.

I don't know what either Pamela or I could have done other than stand fast. I decided to postpone truth.

In about five minutes we could see the outlines of a sleek white Coast Guard cutter in the fog.

"Over here! Over here!" I yelled frantically.

"Here! Here! Here!" yelled Pamela Yew.

The cutter hove to about twenty-five yards away; I could

hear the plop of a small boat hitting the water. The coast guardsmen, given their pick, lifted Pamela from the water first. She was fetching, what with her clothes plastered to her skin. Then they fished me out, a fool with his teeth chattering.

I was met on the cutter by Clint Johns.

"You!" he said.

"Me," I admitted. The coast guardsmen were falling over themselves trying to help Pamela Yew. They ignored me. Compared to her, I had the attraction of a leper.

"How the hell?" asked Johns.

"Hammond pushed us. What are you doing out here? Not that I'm not grateful."

"Following the ferry with sonar equipment in case Hammond dumped something over for a boat pickup. Your struggling bodies made two neat little pips on our sonar screen."

I decided not to tell Johns about the Fiat switch. As long as I had thing mineral, Leanne Armstrong was safe. Besides that, Johns was in no mood to be told the heroin business had been nonsense from the beginning.

I could take some pleasure in the episode. I had to smile when I imagined the expression on Hammond's jubilant face when he broke into the trunk of the rented Fiat.

Pamela Yew looked pretty funny also, when she emerged on deck wearing a sailor's outfit two times too large for her.

She looked at me, closed her eyes, and shook her head sadly. "You're a real he-man, John Denson; a woman feels safe around you. Did you know that?"

I laughed like a screwball because it felt good to be alive. "I would have pulled a fancy judo stunt and flipped him over the edge, only I was waiting for you. Didn't want to patronize you."

Pamela Yew laughed also. "Well next time, Mr. Denson, you go right on ahead."

Eighteen

CLINT JOHNS RADIOED AHEAD and Pamela Yew and I had a taxi waiting for us at the wharf. We walked ashore in sailor's outfits, holding bundles of wet clothes.

"Well, Pamela, would you like to stay with me to the end, or would you like to be taken back to your apartment? I think you've lost the bet."

"Lost the bet?" She shook her head. "Not until you show me thing mineral, Mr. Denson. I'll stay with you. I don't want to miss out on the fun."

I gave her a lewd grin. "I guarantee you won't miss out on that."

"Save the clever lines until you've won the bet." She had a way about her that made me wonder where I'd gone wrong.

"No reason why you shouldn't come along," I said.

"Okay if the cab circles by my apartment so I can change into some different clothes?"

When we got back to my place, Pamela watched "Masterpiece Theater" on the tube while I settled down in a hot bath. I wasn't in the tub for five minutes when the phone rang. With a towel around my middle I trailed water through the hall and answered it. Pamela leaned to one side as though she were trying for a peek.

"Denson?" a man asked. Hammond.

I could hear street noises in the background. He was speaking from a phone booth. "Me," I said.

"What did you do with my goods, Denson?" He was enraged. No, enraged is not quite accurate.

"They're safe."

"I want them."

"I imagine you do. I want the young woman, Leanne. I want her alive and intact." I needed thing mineral to win my bet. I needed thing mineral to keep Leanne Armstrong from a sadist. Bluff time.

"No cops or she's dead," said Hammond.

"No cops."

Hammond gave me the address of an all-night diner. "Be there at one a.m. Park your car across the street and come across alone. The girl will be sitting in the diner. Leave the goods. Bring the keys and you can have the girl. I'll drive it away and it'll be done."

"Sounds too much like our last get together."

"That's the way it is if you want the girl alive and with her nose still on her face."

"It's a deal," I said quickly.

"What will you be driving?"

I put my hand over the receiver. "Pamela, may I borrow your BMW tonight? I need it to con Leanne Armstrong away from Hammond." Pamela nodded yes. "A silver BMW," I said. "Your goods'll be in the trunk."

"Be there or I'll send you her nose in a paper bag," he said.

"I'll be there."

Hammond hung up.

Pamela arched one eyebrow. "Do you know how much the 'goods,' as you call them, are worth?"

I shrugged. "As far as I know, they aren't worth anything more than the price you put on your tail. I don't have them yet anyway; Wayne Phillips will be bringing them over from Port Angeles in the morning."

Pamela closed her eyes and leaned back against my couch.

183

"Why didn't you tell him that on the ferry?" She looked as if she could throw a coffee table at me.

I shrugged. "Bad timing. I was about to but he pushed me over the side."

"You stupid jackass!"

"Oh, come on. Let's not have our first fight now."

"You could have had us killed!"

"We're still alive, Ms. Yew. You're going to have to be a lot more friendly than this if you're going to honor your end of the bet. It'll be the womanly thing to do."

Pamela smiled. "I haven't seen thing mineral yet."

"You will." I called Tony Butterfield, who was coordinating the net from the FBI office.

"You people find your heroin yet?"

There was a pause. "No, but we will."

"Well, Hammond called. He's willing to swap me Leanne Armstrong for ten thousand dollars at one a.m."

"What?"

"I said Hammond is willing to swap Leanne Armstrong for ten grand."

"Where would a flake like you raise that kind of money?"

"I've got a painting by a nineteenth-century artist named Eakins that's worth five times that. A phone call to any number of people who know I own it and I get my money."

"You want to make the switch?"

"Yes. I want the girl."

"You make it and we'll be on his ass like a bad smell. You'll get your money back. Guaranteed."

I let out a lungful of air. "Thank you Mr. Butterfield. Do you suppose you could fix my BMW with a homing device?"

"Come by at midnight and we'll fix you up."

"Later, then."

"Later."

I hung up.

Pamela Yew looked at me in disbelief. "You're a hell of a liar, do you know that?"

I grinned. "Everybody underestimates a flake. I count on it. It's part of my act, has been for years. It's how I survive." I gave a grand gesture. "Self-deprecation, that's the trick. Put yourself down. Give 'em a shrug. Give 'em a grin. Give 'em a leer. Lead with the obvious. Lulls 'em."

"And you win in the end."

I shrugged and grinned.

It was raining when we left for the FBI garage. It was a cold rain, a steady downpour. Pamela and I listened to the rain while Butterfield installed the homing device.

"You're not going to take her with you, are you?"

"She's an adult. She wants to go, she goes."

Butterfield shook his head. "Women!"

"She can do a job, believe me."

"Uh, huh." He didn't believe me.

I pulled Pamela's BMW to the side of the road two blocks shy of the rendezvous. I leaned back and looked across at her good brown eyes. "Listen, I don't mean to be patronizing, but it doesn't make much sense for both of us to go strolling up there. Hammond expects only me. I've got to con him into thinking thing mineral is waiting for him in the trunk of this car."

Pamela blinked once. "And what do you think I should do?"

"I think you should ease up toward the diner in the shadows and be ready to blow him off the map if he tries anything. Have you ever killed a man before?"

"No," she said.

"Do you think you can now?"

"Yes," she said.

I believed her.

I let Pamela out and continued slowly down the street. I parked the BMW across the street from the diner and sat there for a few minutes. There was one customer in the diner. A girl. She looked like Leanne but I couldn't be sure. I stepped out of the BMW and crouched by the front end, wondering if I should go immediately across the street. I thought not. Better to check it out first.

I walked away from the diner and turned into the first alley I came to and looked back. The eatery looked for all the world like the famous painting by Edward Hopper, portraying a few lonely patrons in such an establishment. People surrounded by concrete and brick. The street in both directions was poorly lit. The only illumination came from yellow street lamps. The rain kept falling. I could see a waitress behind the counter give Leanne a refill on a cup of coffee. There she sat, waiting. I still wasn't sure. I circled up the block through an alley and checked the street from another angle. Nothing. I could hear the water gurgling into the storm drains. I could hear the distant thunder of a truck on the interstate highway. Then just the water again. I could hear it echoing in the tunnels beneath the streets. I slipped back through the alley, keeping tight against one side. I went two blocks in the other direction, hoping Pamela Yew was being equally cautious. I eased at last into the street. Still nothing. My shoes had seen better days; my feet were soaked from the water. I returned to my original corner and watched the diner for several minutes before making my decision. It was clear.

I started trotting across the street; the water in my shoes made a rythmic squish, squish, squish. When I was fifteen feet from the curb, Leanne turned and looked at me from inside.

Black eyes.

She had black eyes and a puffy face. Her lips were split sausages. She wasn't Leanne. She was Linda. Out of the hospital. I would never understand her decoys. But there she was, helping Jerry Hammond lure me across the street.

I didn't have anything to swap. Hammond didn't either.

Hooves and horns! Hammond's .357. Hollow points! Sweet Jesus!

I turned and began to sprint.

I didn't hear the first shot booming from the darkness of the alley next to the diner. The white-hot slug ripped into my thigh; I went down hard on the wet pavement, skidding wildly on my face. I rolled crazily, knowing instinctively that I had to make a hard target in order to survive.

I was on my feet, still sprinting in spite of the pain.

I heard the boom of Jerry Hammond's pistol again and a third time.

He missed both times.

186

Then I was out of range and the shooting stopped. It was still raining. I could feel the warmth of the blood on my leg. I kept running. The pain! The pain! The pain! I could hardly stand it. I turned a corner, still going full tilt. I didn't go another fifteen yards when my leg collapsed and I pitched sideways and rolled down some stairs leading to the basement of an ancient apartment building.

The red brick stairs nearly tore the skin off the side of my face on the way down.

I was still conscious at the bottom. My leg was sticky with hot blood that kept coming and coming and coming. I didn't know how to stop it. Then I heard the footsteps. I looked up:

Hammond. He grinned and eyed me down the barrel of his .357. "Christ man, you gotta be the biggest damned fool I ever met. A sucker from the word go."

I suppose he was right at that.

Hammond cocked the revolver.

I watched, expecting never to hear the sound of the shot that killed me. John Denson died with his fly zipped and his eyes open. I heard the shot all right.

And wound up with Jerry Hammond in my lap missing most of his skull.

Pamela Yew appeared at the stairwell. She put her pistol back in her handbag. "I killed him, didn't I, Mr. Denson?" Her face was devoid of color. She looked like a stranger for a moment.

"You took most of his head."

"I killed him," she said again.

"Like the television reporters say, he's fatally dead."

"I've never killed anyone before."

I could feel warm blood coming through my fingers. "For what it's worth, no man could have done better. It was a pressure shot."

"That's not what I mean."

"I know what you mean. I've got a severed pumper here. If I don't do something about it, I'll bleed to death."

"Stop it with your thumb, Mr. Denson. I'll get help."

She started to leave but I stopped her with a motion of my

hand. "You know, Pamela, Sam Spade had a secretary. Her name was Effie Perring. She only made his coffee."

Pamela shook her head and smiled. "You're an odd one, John Denson. Thank you." She turned and left.

It wasn't more than a minute later when the wail of sirens began. There must have been dozens of them. Clint Johns was no doubt out there somewhere with a police radio, a George Patton in a green fedora shouting orders to squad cars.

I scooted around on my rump, placed my smashed leg up the stairs, and leaned on the pumper with my thumb. I was wracked with pain that shot upward from my leg and pinned my body against the red brick wall. I wondered how long the enamel on my teeth would hold out. The rain was really coming down.

Nineteen

THE NURSE BROUGHT ME a breakfast of cornflakes, cold scrambled eggs, orange juice, and coffee. My leg was throbbing like a triphammer. I needed another one of those little goodie shots that caused the lovely warm waves to wash across my face. Every four hours, the nurse said. Another two hours to go. She brought me the morning newspaper. Maybe the Super Sonics had gotten it together.

I never made it to the sports pages.

Wayne Phillips had almost one third of the front page to himself. Powell or someone had finagled another two pages on the inside for him. Phillips must have worked his behind off. He had the main story of Jerry Hammond's sting of the FBI plus three sidebars. The best story was Wayne Phillips's account of what happened when he phoned Charlie Grisdale, the special agent in charge of the Bremerton field office and told him he had my Fiat, which was no doubt loaded with the heroin everyone was looking for.

Poor Charlie. He arranged to be at Port Angeles when Phillips left the ferry from Victoria. He also arranged that a rookie Customs officer named Rodney Williamhouse be on hand for the formalities. Charlie wanted the FBI to receive credit for intercepting the shipment of heroin. To make sure the FBI got its due, he insisted that he be on hand when the Fiat was examined in Port Angeles.

Phillips wrote the whole thing in chronological sequence, which was unusual for a news story but a tip to the reader that there was one hell of a kicker coming up.

It was then that Pamela Yew came by for a visit. She had a grin on her face like a Cheshire cat. "Ah, I see you're reading the papers, Mr. Denson. Finished the account of your friend Phillips and the agent Grisdale?"

"Just got started."

Pamela laughed. "Well, you keep reading. How's your leg?"

"They're talking about plastic pins and things like that, but I suppose it'll be all right."

She looked relieved. "That's good to hear. When was your last pain pill?"

"I get shots. Couple of hours ago. Two to go."

"I think I might wait to finish that story if I were you. It might be best to be a bit high."

"You didn't get thing mineral while I was flat on my back with a smashed leg, did you?"

Pamela grinned. "Read on, Mr. Denson."

I read on.

They had opened the trunk first. There was nothing inside the trunk except my clothes and a vase, packed in wads of toilet paper in another suitcase. No more. Grisdale and Williamhouse decided the heroin had to be hidden in the interior of the Fiat, so they dismantled my tires and tore up the upholstery. Nothing. So they tore the Fiat apart almost piece by piece.

Phillips wrote that it was like watching Gene Hackman tear that big Lincoln apart in "The French Connection."

Nothing.

They switched crews and repeated the process.

Nothing.

Grisdale asked Phillips if he remembered me saying anything about a Chinese vase.

Phillips said no.

That was it, said Grisdale. The vase.

The three men—Grisdale, Williamhouse and Phillips—adjourned inside to Williamhouse's office.

There they confronted the ceramic object in the cardboard box.

It was a lovely vase, decorated with stylized jade waterfowl on a tranquil lake graced with amber reeds.

I closed my eyes and looked up at Pamela Yew. "Oh, Christ!"

"What is it?"

"Decoys, Pamela, and flowers."

She looked confused. "I don't understand."

I shook my head and kept reading. There was a delicate mountain behind the lake shrouded by a fine mist, a recurring image in oriental art.

"Damn!"

"Mr. Denson?"

"China," I said.

Grisdale remarked that he had seen such vases on sale in neighborhood flea markets in San Francisco's Chinatown when he was a kid.

Reporter Phillips said it was a beautiful vase. He was wondering what had happened to the painting. He lit a cigarette.

Williamhouse agreed that it was a beautiful vase. This was a big event for him. It could make or break his career.

Phillips had a good sense of drama; he kept the reader going with some nice detail.

Grisdale remarked that the bottom of the vase was thicker than the rest. It was not opaque. He held it up to the light. He couldn't see through the bottom.

Phillips wrote that the puzzled Grisdale chewed pensively on his thumbnail and peered intently into the vase.

I looked up at Pamela.

"Where are you, Mr. Denson?" she asked.

"Grisdale chewing on his thumbnail. The vase, thing mineral, eh, Pamela?"

She nodded yes. "Thing mineral. Keep reading."

Williamhouse remembered that he had read something about a Chinese vase recently. He couldn't remember where. Maybe it was in *Parade* magazine.

191

Grisdale began cleaning the undersides of his fingernails with his bottom teeth.

Phillips said it had been a long day. He was tracing the events in his mind.

Grisdale said it was possible that the heroin story was spread deliberately to divert attention from the vase. He said it was possible the smugglers could have fired ceramic around valuables in the base. Say, gems of some sort. Would that be possible?

Williamhouse deferred to age and experience.

Grisdale asked Phillips's opinion. Phillips said it was his job to report, not think. He sensed disaster. He was trying out some possible leads mentally. Better to have something in mind when you sit down to write under pressure.

Grisdale, without a further word of warning or explanation for his act, abruptly smashed the vase over the edge of Williamhouse's desk.

I looked up at Pamela Yew.

She shook her head and looked pale.

I looked down at Wayne Phillips's one-word paragraph: "Nothing."

Bits and pieces of broken ceramic but nothing else.

Pamela Yew was giggling as I continued. She was following along in her own newspaper.

Phillips reminded Grisdale that the vase belonged to John Denson. What if it didn't have anything to do with Jerry Hammond or smuggling?

Grisdale said the government would buy Denson a new vase. He said Hammond had to be smuggling something.

But what if it was a valuable vase? Phillips asked.

It wasn't, Grisdale assured him.

It was then, it seems, that young Williamhouse's faulty memory returned. His face turned white.

What was it? asked Grisdale.

Williamhouse's memory came in a flood of heartbreaking detail. He opened the top drawer of his desk and pulled out a government memorandum. All Customs agents had received the memo the previous week.

The memorandum, marked urgent, detailed the disappearance, from a Chinese cultural exhibit in Peking, of a priceless Sung dynasty vase. The ceramic ware, called Luan Ch'uan by the Chinese, was made in south China in the twelfth century. It was discovered in an obscure Chinese farmhouse in 1967 and almost immediately disappeared. It reappeared five years later and was made part of a permanent exhibit in Peking. It was then stolen by some talented thieves and, according to sources cultivated by Chinese agents, was taken to Hong Kong. There it remained for another five years, until the thieves let it be known they were willing to part with it for, say, one million dollars. Would the Chinese government be interested? The Chinese stalled. Months passed. The Chinese were certain the vase was within their grasp. Then the Chinese heard rumors that the vase, for reasons not made clear, was to be smuggled to the United States. The Chinese contacted their new friends in Washington.

Could the U.S. Customs people keep an eye peeled? The Chinese translator, who was educated at the University of Kansas, used just that phrase.

Washington agreed.

The memorandum was filled with bureaucratic euphemisms. For those civil servants who are familiar with such language, the meaning was abundantly clear:

Any agent who botched an opportunity to retrieve the vase would pay. He would pay dearly.

The blood drained from Williamhouse's young face. He read the fine print on the memorandum. It was to have been sent to all FBI agents as well.

Why, he asked, had not Grisdale received his copy?

Grisdale, whose pallor now matched that of Williamhouse, sat down and explained. For several days during the previous week, he had not received any mail. One day he got a phone call from Sacramento. The bureau, it seemed, had decided to streamline its mailing procedures. For some unknown reason, Grisdale's mail wound up in Sacramento. The man in Sacramento told him the people in Washington had said the new system, which depended on more efficient computers, would be working smoothly in a few days.

Grisdale told Phillips he had a cousin in Butte. It wouldn't be a bad assignment. Not as good as Puget Sound, but the air was clear and the fishing was good.

Pamela Yew shook her head sadly. "Finished, Mr. Denson?"

Yeah, I was finished. I was laughing so hard my leg ached. "Thing mineral was a vase. A vase!"

"That's it." Pamela Yew was laughing too.

"A two and a half million dollar vase smashed by an FBI agent who didn't get his mail."

"Who didn't get his mail because of a newer, more efficient computer, Mr. Denson."

"The G-men strike again."

"Ahh, yes, but we had a run at it, didn't we, Mr. Denson?"

"We had a run, indeed, Ms. Yew. Only thing was, I thought we were after a painting."

"I know you did."

I couldn't believe it. "Neither of us won."

"It's kind of too bad in a way; an ending would have been nice."

I held up a hand. "Now wait a minute. If nobody won, you're right, there's no ending. But look at it another way· we both lost. Losers pay up, don't they?"

"It doesn't work that way, Mr. Denson, not at all."

"Think about it."

"It wouldn't be an even swap."

"I don't understand."

Pamela Yew looked outside at the rain falling over Seattle. "I suppose it wouldn't hurt me to tell you the truth, would it?"

"It wouldn't be a bad idea."

"That was a lie about me being married ten years. I was married for four. I was frigid, Mr. Denson. I couldn't stand to touch my husband. I had known him for ten years, that's so. He was my high school sweetheart. Everybody expected us to get married one day; there was no question." She paused.

"So what was the problem?"

"The problem was there was no passion. I didn't love him. He told me I wasn't sexy. He wouldn't let me wear makeup. He wouldn't let me wear anything that looked halfway attractive.

He talked to my mother about it, Mr. Denson, and she asked me if maybe I wasn't attracted to women."

"This lasted for four years?"

"Four years, Mr. Denson. A sexless marriage for four years. When I caught him in bed with a friend of ours, I knew it was time. I left."

My leg was beginning to throb again. I turned in the bed. "So why did you become a hooker?"

"To prove myself, maybe, I don't know. I had a girlfriend who was making a lot of money working out of a hotel and she said why not? I agreed. Why not? Maybe I would learn about sex."

"Did you?"

Pamela Yew laughed bitterly. "Oh, I found out about sex, okay. I got this."

"I suppose you went to a shrink, all that."

"All of that. It's a mental thing; there's nothing wrong with me physically. My psychiatrist said the first step was to find a man I can talk to."

"I'm a listener, always have been. I've learned a lot from you already."

She smiled. "Thank you, Mr. Denson. Suffice it to say that, barring a miracle, you'd have been disappointed had you won our bet."

"Well, I don't know," I said.

"We'll never know, will me?"

"I still say we should declare ourselves both losers and pay up."

"You're a kind man, Mr. Denson, but we've been through that. Nobody won. It's done now. Is there anything else you'd like to know?"

"Jerry Hammond."

"I was one of his girls, got paid a hundred bucks for a ten-minute pop. Jerry Hammond was a pimp but he didn't murder anybody, like Bobby Carroll did. He turned to killing later. Hammond did run a string of high-priced call girls like Carroll."

"One night he skipped town with a wad."

Pamela Yew grinned. "Well done. That's exactly what he

195

did, following a convention in San Francisco of the American Bar Association. The women of Coyote were right after him, of course. The problem was he spent the wad before they could run him down."

"So they've been watching for him to make a score so they could get their money back."

"Right again. When they got onto the vase business they turned to me immediately because of what he'd done to me. They offered me half of the vase's price if I could pull a snatch."

"So you came up with the Jay Hamarr revenge story to get you a little free help."

"I needed somebody to do my work for me in Cayuse. A woman detective just doesn't walk into an out-of-the-way place like that and start asking questions. The people who live there just aren't ready for it. I also wanted somebody to help me out in Seattle, somebody who knew the town and had connections with the police. I wanted a story that was close to the truth but didn't implicate me personally."

"You knew I would crack your Jay Hamarr story."

"If you were any good, Mr. Denson, and people said you were. I helped you along by asking about Seattle when the dentist had his hands in your mouth."

I had to laugh at that. "I knew for sure something was phony when you wouldn't go to Hammond's house with me."

"When you knew I was lying I expected you to go for whatever it was you thought Hammond was smuggling."

"I went for it."

"And made a foolish bet in the bargain. A little extra for me, I'll have to admit. I also never expected you to pay off, Mr. Denson."

"You planned all along on taking it from me with your Beretta."

"All the easier because you don't carry a weapon. I'd been told that before I went to see you. I was passive, Mr. Denson, because men expect women to be passive. They think nothing of it."

"Which leaves unanswered the question of how Coyote got onto the vase, Ms. Yew."

"Your cute little Leanne Armstrong was a graduate assistant to Dr. John Palmer here at the University of Washington. Few people in the world knew more about Asian art than Palmer. The idea of that priceless vase floating loose in the Hong Kong underworld fascinated him. He discussed it with his graduate assistants one night at a party. Leanne Armstrong's escort pumped him about it. Palmer didn't think much about it until a month later when he saw the young man's picture in the newspaper: Jerry Hammond, arrested on smuggling charges that were later dropped."

I tried to remain patient. "Okay, okay. But what I want to know is how word got to Coyote?"

"I'm coming to that. Palmer began to wonder about Hammond's interest in the vase and said so to Dr. John Hsiu at a professional meeting in Denver."

"And Dr. Hsiu?"

"And Dr. Hsiu, love, told it to a hooker in San Francisco. Some are talkers and we whores are everywhere listening."

"I still say we should call it an even swap."

She looked at me like I was nuts and shook her head. "I've got a case waiting for me in San Francisco. I'm sorry I can't stay. But when you're up and about give me a call, John Denson."

"Then the bet's not finished."

"I didn't say that." She leaned over and gave me a kiss.

"I never did ask you about your last name. I'm curious. What's the origin of Yew?"

Pamela Yew laughed. "I was married to a Jackson, as in Andrew. I'm neither a Jack, as you can see, nor a son. So I changed it."

"To a tree."

"They make bows out of yew, Mr. Denson. An extraordinary wood; it bends but it won't break." She snapped her fingers' with a loud pop. "It comes back just like that."

She had a long, gorgeous spine. She bent, gave me another light kiss, and was gone without looking back.

So there it was: Pamela Yew had planned from the start for me to do her work for her both in Cayuse and Seattle. She used the Jay Hamarr story for a decoy and I went for it to the point of betting my Thomas Eakins after I found she was lying. Jerry Hammond sensed that I was morally obliged to find Leanne Armstrong for her sister. He used the women to decoy me into doing his smuggling for him.

I returned to Phillips's account of the fiasco but my heart wasn't in it. Linda told the police how she had tried to tell me about the vase from her hospital bed. She said her mind was fuzzy at the time from drugs. All she could remember were the funny ducks. She had run across a photograph of the vase, she said, when she was washing her husband's trousers. The picture was in a hip pocket. She said the ducks didn't look right so she concluded they were decoys. Her father hunted water-fowl, she said. He would never have laid a spread of such dumb-looking decoys.

When I finished with the paper I threw it across the room. It was time for my morphine and my leg hurt like hell.

Twenty

EVENTUALLY THE DOCTORS PICKED the pieces of bone and lead from my leg. I spent another month eating bland food and staring at the rain and the hospital parking lot. My mother drove up once a week to see me, but that wasn't the kind of visitor I needed. Phillips and Powell came by occasionally. Phillips was always drunk and always had a pint of something to slip me. One time he brought me a skin magazine but that made things worse. I lay there in the semidarkness and listened to the nurses in the hall talk about their love life. Every once in a while somebody would scream in the night instead of pressing the call button.

My doctor had an Italian name and needed a haircut. That made me suspect him right away. One day I told him I owned a Fiat that needed tuning all the time. He didn't say anything. I think he knew I was onto him. I was constipated and my leg was so sore that for weeks it almost hurt to blink or swallow.

I was released from the hospital after a month. The first thing I did was go to my office and take my Eakins from the wall. It was a nice enough painting but no big deal unless you knew it was painted by Thomas Eakins. Philistine that I am, I had to admit that I'd seen a lot of paintings by sidewalk

199

artists I liked just as well. It meant something to Pamela Yew, who was an artist.

She wanted it enough to put her butt on the line for it.

She saved my face from Hammond's cowboy boots in Cayuse.

She saved my life when Hammond was ready to take me out with his .357 Magnum. She had to kill him to do it.

It's not easy to kill someone. I know I couldn't do it, which is why I don't carry a weapon. I was ordered to kill a man once when I was in the intelligence service. He was a Brit who had spied on his American cousins. The Americans were annoyed but they didn't complain; there's no discipline in that. The thing to do was waste him, teach the Brits some manners. I was the hit. I tailed him one afternoon, found he had blue eyes and a brown mustache with white hairs in it. I broke into his flat too, found he didn't use shoe trees and his worn oxfords needed polishing.

I had been trained twice, once at Fort Holabird, Maryland, by Army Intelligence, once at Peary, Virginia, by the Central Intelligence Agency. I was second in my class at the Bird. The instructors at Peary thought I was an ace.

I left the Brit's flat and told my station chief I wouldn't do the hit. The station chief, a small, precise man named Adrian Kile, sniffed once and told me, "That's it, Denson. Go home."

I did and wound up a newspaper reporter in Honolulu.

I crated the painting, drove to the post office, and mailed the crate to Pamela Yew. I had an idea she wouldn't keep it. If she did, I didn't care. I walked away from the clerk with no regrets.

Then I got into my Fiat and headed for Cayuse for a rest. I limped like Walter Brennan in those old movies but had been assured by the Italian's superior, a handsome middle-aged surgeon, that it would go away in time. He had been watching a nurse walk by when he told me, which wasn't reassuring somehow. On top of that he picked his nose furtively on his way out of my room. He saw that he'd been caught and looked foolish. Surgeons don't pick their noses.

When I got back to Sandy Johnson's bar three days later, it

was as though I had never left. Jim Sullivan sat on the same stool he was on the night Jerry Hammond punched Linda. He had a shot of Jim Beam in his hand as always. Straight up. Water back.

"What'll it be, John?" asked Sandy. I could have just gone out for a hamburger instead of being the principal actor in a now much-discussed shootout.

"Make it a Blitz," I said.

"How's your leg?"

"Bit of a limp still."

Sullivan looked concerned but didn't say anything. He polished off his whiskey to show his concern. He did care, Sullivan did. It wouldn't have been manly to make a fuss.

"Christ, I'll bet that hurts," he said.

"Not so much. Mostly I have to get some muscles built up again. The doctors say most of it will get squared away."

"Your old man said it hit a bone," said Sandy.

"They were able to weld the bone together with plastic. Used to be they'd put a pin in there. This is a lot better."

"Say, Denson, I got a letter back from the Federal Wildlife Commission," said Sullivan.

I couldn't remember right off what he was talking about.

"You remember, one of those geese I shot that day was tagged. I never did get to tell you what happened."

"Hell, let's hear it," I said. "Another beer, Sandy."

"My old lady picked and cleaned the bastards but the one that had been tagged was so shot up he was worthless. You should have seen him: scars all over him. I got curious so I waded into the sucker with my hunting knife while I watched a ball game on the tube. I counted two hundred and sixteen shot in his breasts, wings, and innards before I gave up. The old lady was complaining about goose guts on the floor."

"Christ!" said Sandy. He could have been talking about the two hundred and sixteen shot or the goose guts. His comment was noncommital.

"Bullshit!" I said.

"That's a fact." Sullivan enjoyed a story like this. "I bet the count would have gone closer to three hundred but by that time he was so shredded up I couldn't see what I was doing. Just shredded meat."

"You sent the tag to the wildlife people?"

"Got an answer back a week ago. One of those government forms. Had everything except his sex life. He was tagged three years ago in Canada and was penned three times since, twice in Mexico and once in Thule Lake, California. The game people decoy them into pens and check for tags. Saw a thing about it on television."

"Three times," I said.

"I sent along a note with the tag telling them the carcass shot-count. One of their people bucked along a note with the bird's personal history form. The note said there have been geese killed that carried over four hundred shot."

"Might as well eat a gravel pit," I said.

"Damndest thing I ever saw," said Sullivan. He motioned for another whiskey. "The shotgun shells are just useless if a goose can fly to Mexico with four hundred shot in his innards. You can bring them in over a perfect spread and blast the living shit right out of them. They just take it and keep going. You might draw a couple of feathers for your trouble but that's all. It's just damned near impossible to bring them down." Sullivan shook his head.

He was right, of course. Everything and everybody wants to live. Pamela Yew was loaded with shot but she kept flying.

I didn't feel like thinking about it any longer. I limped back to the cafe next door for some breakfast. I didn't have a chance to place my order when Sandy Johnson came in to tell me I had a long distance phone call. The woman was waiting on the line.

"Has a good, rich voice." He grinned.

"Oh, yeah?"

"She wanted to know how your leg is?"

"Did you ask which one?" I laughed.

Sandy held the door open for me. "Yes, I did as a matter of fact."

202

"What did she say?"

"I think she has a dirty mind. She laughed and said they all count?"

"And what did you say?"

"I said as far as I know they're all in working order."